Small Worlds

A collaborative anthology of short stories and poetry

Published in Great Britain 2014

by the University of Brighton Literary
Society

brightonuls@gmail.com

Contents

Foreword by Isabel Ashdown, Writer in Residence at the University of Brighton

When I was first told of the 2014 anthology theme – Small Worlds – I knew we would be in for a treat. Because the idea of Small Worlds seemed to me to present such diverse scope for creative thought, and indeed the submissions this year were rich and original. Among the entries, we see the literal use of the expression, in small towns, enclosed rooms, on lost islands; there are the internal spaces, in the fallible workings of the human body and mind; and the abstract worlds, equally fascinating, in which inanimate objects are given life, or thought, to observe on the places to which they are bound.

The American film director John Huston is quoted as saying, 'The directing of a picture involves coming out of your individual loneliness and taking a controlling part in putting together a small world.' The same could perhaps be said for the art of creative writing: in imagining these fictional landscapes, the writer must venture from the safety of their own small world to bravely strike out and create something new, something that perhaps reflects elements of the larger world that others might recognise.

In a technological age increasingly lived out under the glare and white noise of social networks and the wider global community, it is no wonder that so many seek out the private spaces to be found in reading and writing. Words, whether we're absorbing them or creating them, can speak to us as individuals, for our own unique interpretations, within our own small worlds. This compilation of short stories, poems and flash fiction will, I

1

am sure, provide many readers with much solitary pleasure
and diversion.

I regularly advise writers and students on the importance
of competitions and publications in their early writing
careers. A publication track record shows potential agents
and publishers that you mean business; that you are a
writer. Congratulations to all who entered the competition
and contributed to this book. The standard was high, and
so, for me, the process of selecting winners was an
enjoyable one.

Finally, on behalf of the readers and writers of Small
Worlds, sincere thanks are due to the dedicated individuals
who masterminded the submissions process, skilfully
selected a shortlist, and ultimately brought the collection to
life. To Dr Jessica Moriarty, Course Leader for English
Language and Literature; to Ellie Exton, Sophie Lloyd-
Catchpole and the wider editorial team for the Brighton
University Literary Society – thank you.

Isabel Ashdown

This year's prizes were awarded by Isabel Ashdown, Author and Writer in Residence for the University of Brighton.

First prize was awarded to:

'The Witches' by Ruby Speed.

The runner-up prizes were awarded to:

'10 minutes 1000 words' by Nadja Jepsen and **'Wardrobe in a Hotel Room' by Miriam Davies**.

The following entries were shortlisted for prizes.

'Jellywasps!' by James Novis

'Wait here' by Jessica Green

'Leaving Ometepe' by Christopher Sciacca

'Depth' by Will Bamber

'Shadows' by Clare Brown

'Abjection' by Abi Jolley

'Shallot'by by Maria Wallingford

'TABOO²' by Gemma Burford

'Waiting for Something to Happen' by Jenny Harding

Cover Image by Véronique Freyer

The Witch

by Ruby Speed

There exists, somewhere, an island with no name which from above seems like an emerald shining a luminous green into the sea-sky. No humans live there, but the jungled forest is full of Witches. The rubber trees on the island live a thousand years, translucent-purple caterpillars as fat as a baby's arm crawl over moss-covered rocks and tiny deadly flies flicker between pools of white light. Under the vast, dense camouflaged leaves, the forest air is suffocatingly hot and sweat-inducing; you can lose your breath there and never find it again. Deep in the heart of the forest corpse flowers hide intricate, colourful and delicious mushrooms for the Witches to eat, but no humans have ever tasted them. They are horrified by the flowers' stench of decaying flesh and most flee in horror back to their ships, although it is only a very small number who have ever made it so far into the jungle. Humans are such frightened and stupid little creatures; not many of them have even gazed upon the island. Those who have, return home not with a Witch's head on a stick, nor stolen exotic spices or fruits, nor impossibly beautiful but silent wives, as they vowed they would, but only with stories and warnings from 'Witch Island' and less men than they started their voyages with. The children of the adventurers listen wide eyed, and some won't sleep for weeks.

Do not think that the Witches are evil, they are not. They did not choose to be Witches any more than you chose to be human, and Witches are the only things they know how to be. And just as the adventurers tell their sons stories to warn them of Witches, the Witches tell their daughters stories to warn them of humans. Both humans and Witches fear the other more than anything, but for very different reasons. Adventurers' children are afraid of the Witches' supernatural powers, their sharp teeth and wits. But there are legends which say that if a human boy can make a Witch fall in love with him, she will be transformed from a Witch into a beautiful doll-bride, and that is what all the little Witches were terrified of.

There was one little Witch on the island who had power over all natural things; from conjuring tiny flowers to controlling the forest's oldest trees and fiercest beasts. Her name was Novi, and her mother was the chief Elder Witch. She was the most beloved and cherished child on the island; a little Witch Princess. On the day of her birth, the other Elder Witches showered the child with gifts; animals to eat with her tiny pointed teeth, a crown made from twisted twigs and the blood of a sacrificed beast which she was to drink. She lived a perfect life, until one day when Novi was little more than a child, and she walked by herself in the heart of the forest. She often wandered alone around the Island, but was forbidden to venture into the centre of the jungle, as her mother warned her:

"If a human finds you in the deepest depths of the forest, they will try to kill you and no one will hear your calls through the trees."

But Novi was forgetful and distracted; a happy and brave young Witch who often disobeyed her mother's many rules. Novi played with the pond of water in the very centre of the island, forging little moving figures from the water then watching them melt back into the turquoise pool. A bird cried in the distance. The sun burned her neck.

And she heard a sound. It did not sound like any bird or insect or creature she had heard before. She paused, with small plants growing silently around her feet. She waited, hunched over, like a tiger waiting to pounce. Nothing happened. She threw a rock into the bushes nearby, and then heard a voice, unlike any she'd heard before.

The voice spoke in a similar language to her, but it spoke in simplistic sentences. She knew it to be the voice of a human invader.

"I···mean...no···harm," said the voice in a slow, stupid way. "You···" said the human coming out from his hiding place and pointing at Novi, "are very···beautiful···Understand? Beautiful?"

6

Novi stood still where she was, she knew humans were cunning and evil, and knew this boy was pretending to be stupid. She said nothing and frowned at him.

"You," he said pointing again, "do amazing things⋯with the water⋯very clever tricks"

"Thank you," she replied reluctantly, "but it's not actually a trick."

"Will you show me?" he moved closer "Can you do it again?"

"Of course I can," Novi retorted, "but you must stay over there where you are."

The human boy seemed to understand as he stood still, waiting Novi regarded him for a moment then continued her water-conjuring. Whilst she did this the boy thought to himself: *What a beautiful and strange girl- I will make her my wife.*" Novi had her back turned to the boy now, and concentrated on her little liquid sculptures. The boy approached her silently and took a ring with a tiny red diamond out of his pocket. He had heard the stories too, about Witches turning into good brides, and his father had given him this ring and claimed it would melt any Witch's heart and make her fall in love. Before Novi could push him away, the boy grabbed her hand and stuck the ring onto her finger. Novi screamed as she saw the ring on her finger, and felt herself start to transform. She felt her skin melt away, and was sure she was becoming a speechless doll-bride. But she looked down at her hands, now covered with thick brown fur. She growled. The boy shrieked and looked up at the bear which now towered above him. She ate him in one mouthful.

By Ruby Alice Speed, a short feminist from Nottingham who is obsessed with Witches

10 Minutes 1000 Words

by Nadja Jepsen

Ten million people reside in the megacity of Seoul, South Korea.

8:00am

The alarm startles Lucy awake with a jolt. She feels ambushed, just like yesterday morning and the morning before that. She has woken up at eight for the past nine weeks but her sleep pattern is not routine. Ever since she stepped off the plane into the Incheon International Airport in in Seoul her anxiety and insomnia have flourished. She knew immediately that she had made a mistake coming to Korea to teach English. In the past nine weeks she realized: she didn't like children, she didn't like teaching and she didn't like cold weather. Historically, she wasn't an impulsive person but three months prior when she got a job offer, spontaneity seemed great. But now, with ten months to go, she feels regret.

8:01am

Jae sits in the waiting room of his English academy. He is waiting for his morning class with Jonathan, his teacher from New Zealand. During their last class Jonathan told Jae that he was a "Kiwi" which Jae found simultaneously funny and confusing. A brown, furry fruit? When Jae had gone home, searched online, and according to the internet, a Kiwi was "a common nickname for people from New Zealand". He learned that a kiwi is also a flightless bird. He is excited to address Jonathan by the nickname when class starts any second now.

9

8:02am

SoYoung is lying on her couch, where she slept last night. She has been awake for about an hour and her alarm won't go off for another 40 minutes. This is the third time that she has slept on the couch since November. She sleeps on the couch when her boyfriend Mitch drinks too much and starts acting like an asshole, which seems to be more frequent these days. In the garbage can, under an empty bag, is a long letter she wrote to him. He won't ever know it was there.

8:03am

Hyuk is running down the steps two at a time at Gongdeok station. He overslept again. He needs to catch the 8:04 train or he will surely miss his connection. Mr. Kim, his boss, doesn't like him and blatantly looks for excuses to reprimand him. He has only been working at Shinhan for a few months and he really can't be late. The woman in front of him is walking slowly down the steps and swaying from side-to-side, making it impossible to pass. The devastating melody of the subway doors chimes.

8:04am

Tom is standing on the subway with the majority of his weight resting on his right foot. The train is packed and an old Korean man has positioned himself right under Tom's left arm. As the train jerks and stops Tom worries that he will bump into the tiny man and knock him over. Tom knows if this happens he will look like a "rude American". He's not American, but everyone always assumes he is. If he knew more Korean he couldn't easily explain where he was from, maybe he'll take a class next semester, but maybe not. He watches the stops pass as the nerves in his foot start to tingle.

8:05am

Soo-a is sitting on the subway and scrutinizing her face in her compact mirror. She just got back from two years in Canada, where she studied English and worked at a café in Vancouver. Canada was okay but she was really homesick. The first thing her mother said to her when she got back was "You need to sign up for a gym. You have gotten so fat!" Soo-a holds the mirror at various angles looking for the most flattering perspective.

8:06am

Sophie is looking at her boyfriend, Brendan, through her computer screen. They are having one of their bi-weekly Skype conversations. Brendan and Sophie started dating right before she left to Korea but they decided to stay together while she was gone. Brendan is telling her about an old man he saw at the beach that was trying to change from his wet swimsuit to his dry clothes but while he was changing the wind blew his towel away. Sophie spills a little coffee while she laughs.

8:07am

Bus no.3, full of kindergarteners, arrives at the English Time preschool in Sinchon. The bus driver mechanically pulls into the spot adjacent to the front door as a symphony of giggles and gibberish fill the bus. It's Wednesday so all the kids are wearing their matching blue and yellow gym outfits. They like gym class because they get to run around and play games. Most Wednesdays, on the ride home, the kids excitedly talk nonstop about the activities in gym class.

8:08am

Angel Coffee is opening eight minutes late today. Usually the scaffolding is up by 7:55 and the doors are open by

8:00. One regular has already left for work and will have to stop at her second favourite coffee shop but two others are waiting somewhat impatiently by the door. They scoff about the belated access while the shy employee bows his head and quickly starts making their customary drinks.

8:09am

Alice is sitting at Incheon International Airport and waiting for her connecting flight to Kuala Lumpur, Malaysia. She is tired and annoyed at her long layover but she is pleased that the Korean airport offers free wifi. She absentmindedly looks at her watch, she technically has enough time to take the subway into the city and see some attractions in Seoul while she is here. Her adventurous side wants to put her luggage in a locker and go see Namsan Tower that is displayed in various pictures around the airport, but her lazy side wants to get a coffee and go to the airport movie theatre and kill time.

Nadja grew up in California and moved to Seoul, South Korea to teach English for three years after she graduated from university. She is currently studying MA Education.

Wardrobe in a Hotel Room

by Miriam Davies

I am of dead wood
dried to stop the rot
sliced with precision to fit a purpose
painted with another skin.
I stand in a seasonless
weatherless room
against a cream coloured wall
and I wonder what it is like
to be able to see stories unfold for more than just one night
to see beginnings and ends
not just pauses between someone else's days
to watch giants become giants
to witness greats falling
and new growth rising.
Although I do not have the memories
of the youths of my dead limbs
of competing for light as they left the soil
even though I have never breathed
never soaked up building blocks out of the air
nor reached to extreme depths in search of water
and even though I know nothing
of the embrace of ivy
of frost on my skin
of the brush of the wind
sometimes I think the sycamore outside the window
waves to me as if I am his brother
and in those moments I think I can imagine well
the taste of sunlight
the coolness of dark soil
the standing with a thousand others

our epic unfolding.
Stand me there on the ground and let me sink with the
leaves
return me to where I've never been.

Miriam is a postgraduate student at the University of Brighton. She spends a lot of time writing songs to play at open mic nights and has recently become interested in poetry. She had her first poem published last year in the University of London's anthology In Protest.

Waiting for Something to Happen

by Jenny Harding

Sheepdip Road is not strictly a road because it doesn't lead anywhere. It continues a short distance and disappears into an impenetrable thicket, beyond which is open countryside. There is nothing much out there unless you have an affinity with sheep. Some people do.

One morning I stepped outside my front door at Sixty Three, intending to go somewhere, when I was confronted by a trench in middle of Sheepdip Road! Yes, a trench! It had appeared overnight.

I scanned Sheepdip Road for a way round the trench. There was no way round. It ran all the way to the impenetrable thicket. It was too wide to jump over and would have been deep enough to drown in if it was full of water, which it wasn't.

The doors of our bare brick terraced houses open right onto a brick cobbled pavement. Dandelions wait in the cracks between the cobbles for something to happen.

Opposite the row of houses is a grass verge, where more dandelions wait. Beyond the verge open countryside stretches all the way to the downs in the distance. A twinkling of sea is just visible where one gentle slope descends and intersects with another that rises in a graceful sweep.

I had placed a bench on the brick cobbled pavement right outside Sixty Three. On summer evenings, I sit there and contemplate the open countryside, the distant hills and the even more distant ocean.

Ingrid at Sixty-Seven plodded out, aided by a floral walking stick. Her eyes were fixed on her feet. She was one hundred years old at least. She had a fine aura of white hair that arranged itself without reference to gravity. She was not dissimilar in appearance to the dandelion clocks that wait in Sheepdip Road for something to happen.

But appearances can be deceptive. Ingrid was not one to wait for things to happen. Instead, she made a round trip to the corner shop every morning. She usually did so without mishap, unless her concentration was broken and she put the wrong foot in front of the other. If that happened, she fell over. That morning, she only got as far as the brick cobbled pavement because the trench was in the way. 'I'll call the Council,' I reassured Ingrid. I pulled out my phone, reported the trench and we waited.

Telegraph poles had been planted at regular intervals along the grass verge. Each pole connected four terraces to the telephone system via black spidery cables festooned across the road.

When it was a windy night I used to lie awake listening to my cable scraping on the roof tiles at Sixty Three. It was a comforting sound. It reminded me that we were connected to as much of the world that exists beyond Sheepdip Road that was in possession of a telephone landline.

A van appeared and a man got out wearing a suit and tie with his trousers tucked in to a pair of wellington boots. He fetched a length of nylon rope, secured one end around the base of a telegraph pole, dropped

16

the other end into the trench and lowered himself until only the top of his head was visible.

'I think you've got a rabbit infestation,' he announced from within the trench.

'Do you mind if I sit down?' Ingrid asked, poking at my bench with her floral walking stick.

'Not at all,' I said.

'This is grand,' said Ingrid, as she eased herself onto the bench and gazed at the view that was framed by a pair of telegraph poles. 'If this is the last thing I ever see I shall die a happy person,' she added.

The man in the trench held up a rabbit by the scruff of its neck. It's ears stuck out at angry angles and its paws thrashed about like overworked knitting needles.

He released the rabbit onto the road on the other side of the trench. It hopped over to the grass verge and ate the waiting dandelions.

'They get disoriented and burrow under the tarmac,' said the man. 'This can compromise the stability of the compacted earth, causing the road surface to collapse in on itself.' While the man delivered this explanation he retrieved and deposited more and more rabbits that also hopped over to eat the dandelions. There were plenty to go round.

The man climbed out of the trench, untied the nylon rope from the telegraph pole and stashed it in the back of his van.

'Tell you what,' he said. 'They're installing fibre-optics in this area. I'll get them to do Sheepdip Road while a handy trench has opened up.'

The man in the van left and returned followed by a truck that transported a fibre-optic installation team. They laid a cable in the trench and connected it to the brick terraced houses.

They dismantled the telegraph poles. 'You won't be needing them anymore,' the man said to us.

Ingrid was admiring the view with her eyes closed. I checked her pulse and peered under her eyelids as the fibre-optic installation team started filling in the trench.

'I think she's gone,' said the man.

'She loved this spot,' I said following Ingrid's close-eyed gaze across the open countryside.

'Tell you what,' said the man. 'We could put her in the trench, right by her favourite view.'

'Yes, I think she would appreciate that,' I said.

We laid Ingrid in the trench. The fibre-optic installation team filled it in and re-surfaced the road.

'Cheerio,' said the man and drove away in his van.

'Cheerio,' said the fibre-optic installation team and drove away in their truck.

'Cheerio,' I said to no one in particular. All was still, quiet and as it should be in Sheepdip Road but I couldn't help thinking that something was missing.

Jenny attended the Creative Writing: Advancing the Craft course in 2013 where she met some great people and got much inspiration. She lives in Lewes with her partner Trevor and works as a manager in the NHS.

Shalott

by Maria Wallingford

Percival T. Fitz-Waterhouse favoured green velvet bowties, pale leather spats and had William Morris wallpaper on his mobile. He saw his neighbours only through the closed-circuit he'd mounted in the guttering. When they found him for the last time he was in a boat full of blood by the weir, naked and minus a penis.

Sure?

Apparently.

Of course everyone knew him, but nobody did. His terrace lay off that road to town, on a concrete islet where the canal slopped and stank. They knew him at the council for his opinions on pavement filth and graffiti. Gossip and suspicion added their bit.

Your voice may have been the last thing he heard. Four hours later they'd dragged him from where he'd floated half a mile. Still a lovely face, they said, a bit of dribble off a cracked last song, otherwise looking charmed by sleep, except that his cock was sliced through with a meat knife and he'd spent a gallon of blood.

Normally I hate to pry but you'll want to know about the beloved Elaine.

Is it a duty to read for more?

19

We can go to Percival's house, not to nick his stuff, but we can rob him of his privacy and the right to be forgotten. We can go in and take something from him that he wouldn't give easily and I'm not talking about either his penis or his spats.

Look at his room. Second-hand mirrors, but so well buffed. Occasional mahogany. A scrap of salvaged marble. He used to wax his bookshelf tops and scrub his inner keyholes with cotton buds.

Clean?

Oh Yes.

Percival T. Fitzwaterhouse. He was named through indulgence, imprudence and deed-poll. He was in love, as spats-wearers would have to be, and the feeling sucked and pumped at him like a well-milked teat.

That love, palpable and painful, he had called Elaine. Look, there on the screen. A face that quells starlight. A mute smile and a thousand hours of airbrushing. He as a miracle worker young Percival. Zoom in. An expert with photo-draughtsmanship, as you see. He could use all the tools, whiskering pixels and grading skin tones, taking out that threatening molecular blemish.

That's what he lived for, a tickle at the far summit of excellence, light-pen and loupe, weaving himself into the web, removing the sickness dot by dot. He found stories in lip-line and the perfect arc of a brow.

His reward came in a tumble of perfect hair and an eye that searched for something improbable beyond the camera's frame. His reward came where she sat first in her autumn coat, patient, perfect, a gateway of melancholy and complex improbability. So alone she might have set the camera up herself.

He'd written to her. There were ways once you'd paid up and signed up. He hung so much on the 'J's of that correspondence, a shapely 'O', a delicately cupped 'u' and a world of exquisite 't's.

From the shadow he found visible kindness and the inability to hurt.

From the menu he found more imagery. Pay per click. Among them some that rewarded and others that punished.

Favoured words: quest, deliverance, protecting.

He buried his chin in his neckwear and gnawed, feeling his own disappointment's persuasive clutch. Sweating palms. Reeling eyes. The ache of idealism gave way, leaving for him the cumbersome residue of longing.

You chose not to know him. Don't blame yourself.

Lonely little tosser. Weirdo. Wanker.

Youth still hummed inside Percival like a failing hard-drive. A half-strangled, guilty moan was a fifteen year old who had grown old on absence.

Read more. Maybe that's why we're here.

Read the headlines never written:

Porn Perv Prangs Penis.

Cock-a-Doodle Doo!

Non-existent headlines. In none of them is he the lover, in none the perfectionist, in none the rescuer. He remains a nothing in headlines that never were.

But his eyes burned with a self-fuelled wish to rescue someone from this.

A rescue. Too lovely, oh, not to be rescued.

Elaine.

He moved with greedy reluctance from those first, wistful portraits that had made a grubby world seem distant. A button open at the neck of her coat. A pale throat and a delicately evolving smile. Oh, Percival, to wait here forever, to leave and to never have been here at all.

But gimme more.

He'd cried to spare her, with a sense that the sparing would at best be only his gaze. He'd repeatedly destroyed his credit cards but had memorised the numbers. His fingers sped automatically through passcode proofs of age and liability until images slipped in and out as though ducking between iron bars in his mind.

To be honest it barely mattered that we'd disturbed him.

Look over at the galley kitchen where, in three paces, his hand seized a blade that could whistle of the slice-iest slice of meat.

You'll know the rest.

Between the aluminium walls and cracked plasma screen, Elaine can guarantee an income from her uncommon smile and a flexible approach to nakedness.

An easy half-hour drop in. Three hundred shots a time, no pressure. The camera responds to her, they say. She chuckles drearily at this, considering it only an intelligent sense of aesthetics and a modicum of muscle control. They're even doing fan mail around it all now and they're wondering about films.

Spitting her gum, she stretches absent-mindedly. The props are ridiculous but, so what- babydoll, fur coat, whatever they're up for. She has plans for the money tonight.

She's off dancing in town, in fact, and gives a compulsive laugh at the turns of all their lives. Her man knows the money's good and has learnt to feel proud. Smile, kiss, giggle. They'll hang out at a club, I guess. Then they'll wander back along a towpath, catch a snog in the shadows and watch the boats float through slabs of electric light. He'll tell her stories in a

secretive murmur and they'll feel an intimacy
that they have no need to share.

TABOO$_2$

by Gemma Burford

Taboo to the power of two: your people say nothing of this.

No-one speaks of two women's love, nobody speaks of
rape,

nor, least of all, of a rape to 'cure' this love

(to show you both what it's like with a 'real man',

to 'correct' your 'twisted' desires, 'straighten' your souls⋯)

a trespass that's always futile, in any case,

if lovers who bleed are bound together by blood,

and if love, in the face of terror, only grows.

I have no right to shout about this; what do I know of your
culture?

I should keep silent. What do I know? I've walked no miles
in your shoes.

I don't understand your ancient traditions. I know it isn't
my place.

I shouldn't impose my values. I mustn't presume. I can't
interfere.

It isn't as if I even knew you. It isn't as if you were here.

Click 'sign', click 'like', and move on. But there's something
in me

that won't forget. There's something to scorch my heart

when I'm lying alone in the dark. What would I do

if I knew your names, if I heard it happen, and saw

the stains of your tears on each other's shoulders? What
would I do

if you lived next door and your children were friends with
mine?

No, the world is small, but not that small. The moment has
gone.

The message went through. What more can I do? Dab at
my eyes,

close the window, return to my day. Shut down. SHUT
DOWN. Move on

*Gemma Burford is a mature PhD student, and a Research
Fellow in Sustainable Development. Her current research
focuses on sustainable design and evaluation. Gemma has
had a passion for creative writing since childhood, and
received the T. S. Eliot Memorial Poetry Prize in 2001
while studying at the University of Kent.*

26

Depth

by Will Bamber

There's a deep groan as the boat heaves us through
the thick, watery blackness of the Arctic Ocean.
We're running at a depth of around one thousand feet
below, and I can feel it. I feel the immense weight of
the ocean wrapping itself around the tiny metal coffin,
the new home that I've been confined to for months
now. I'm steeped in weeks and weeks of unending
darkness, surrounded by dull metal chambers, these
pipes like prison bars, these thin tunnels of flat iron,
the low hum of the nuclear kettle. The endless,
tightening walls, the corridors wrapping around me,
choking me. I'm trapped down a black hole, in a tube
beneath the thick shadow of an empty sea. Travelling
with apprehensive stillness.

A lurid sound calls to me from outside
the boat, drifting through the walls from somewhere
out there in the abyss. I can hear the low murmur
from every room, through every corridor, whatever
I'm doing, whoever I'm with, always inescapably
there. The sound is a pernicious growl, organic but
soulless, rising and falling like breath, slow, constant,
but agitated. I'd never taken any real notice of it
when I first made the vessel my home, after I was
forcibly moved to the service, but as the hours crept
by, skyless, suffocating, stale, the sound became
stronger, and louder, and started to fatten with
urgency. After a while, there wasn't a waking second
that passed where I wasn't agonizingly aware of this
stirring happening out there in the water.

I'm lying on my bunk, the muted
ceiling closing down on me like a lid, listening to the

sound rippling beneath the chatter of the crew around the bunk room. The sound is more than a monotonous drone or a hum – it's like a swarm of muttering noise, a cloud of a million voices moaning together, low and distorted, like chanting from a bottomless hole. I'm pretending to be asleep in my rack, with the bustle of the other men going on around me. Talking, laughing. The dim rumble is rising, louder, and louder, but nobody else seems to notice. Eventually it grows so loud that it drowns out absolutely everything. The sound of my cramped and confined world dissolves. All I hear is a discordant, unnatural noise.

      The bellowing of a huge leviathan, so close, it must be just outside the hull. A cloud of a million screaming voices. The voices hiss and moan and scratch and wail in a violently whirling vapour of sound reverberating from a deep aquatic glottis. I rub my fingers and shiver. The rising of the noise fills a picture in my head, a dark figure looming over the aft of the submarine, a gigantic hive of flesh as big as the sea. A leviathan. A monster. As clearly as I can hear it, I see it in my head. A gurgling scream splits through the lightless brine. The giant, misshapen thing emerges from the abyssal reach of sea and brings its expressionless face down close to the solitary boat. Dead, bloated, children's eyes. The sound rises to pained limits. A cloud of screams. And then a clear utterance, echoed sharply, repeatedly. 'You drowned me, you drowned me.'
Now I'm screaming. No control, just pure animal terror. A broken sweat of guilt. Fear. The familiar gunmetal walls shrink down and constrict the air. The rest of the crew rush over to my bunk, shouting

at me, sounding nearly as terrified as I am. I keep screaming. The sound of my rasping vocal cords mixes with the shouting of the men and the blaring of the leviathan nearby. It's the loudest sound I've ever heard. My ears split. My skull is beaten in. An absolute, gnawing pain. There are hands grabbing at me and holding me down. I hear my name.

'Powell... *Powell*!'

After a few minutes, all the screaming has left me. My throat's too scorched to continue, so instead I'm just sobbing, bleeding tears and clenching my jaw. A dead face in my mind's eye. The sounds from out there in the sea have gone completely silent. I'm back within the stale quiet of the submarine. I feel two hands clasping my face.

'Powell, listen to me.' I hear a voice say – Ensign Seymour. My name, over and over again, punching through the air. I can hear it, but I can't move. I'm boxed in. I'm caged. The clear, dead voice is still repeating in my head. I hear someone shout to get the Commander. I splutter out snot and tears. The stern rivets of the room close down on me and the crowd of men staring down from around my bunk.

A few men remain beside me, but they're blurred, at the edges of my perception. One of them, I think it's Boreham, is grabbing me by the shoulder and talking to me; I'm not sure exactly what he's saying, but I turn to him and look at him. He looks at me. My violent weeping briefly settles, the dim bass of the thing outside still running through the halls. I turn to Boreham and tell him I'm sorry. He says he doesn't know what I'm talking about.

'I'm sorry,' I say, my cheeks quivering, 'I'm sorry.'

There's the sound of heavy footsteps as the Commander walks into the bunk room. I can see him out of the corner of my corroded sight. The room feels the size of a matchbox.

'He's over here.' I hear Boreham call over. The Commander comes over to me, the crew now dispersed, Pearson the medic by his side, stern-faced. The image of a dead face appears in my mind.

'I knew this'd happen,' the Commander sighs, 'there's always one.'

Eight strong arms firmly hold me down. Pearson leans over and I feel a pinch in my shoulder. Waves of cold. Solitude. Blackness.

I'm 22 and do English Literature, I enjoy things like anime and stimulants and imagining what dying will feel like.

Abjection

by Abi Jolley

lil-lets and soiled briefs cradled you
when you needed amniotic warmth
twelve week scan captured in the PHS

ejected clusters of dead cells
stain the cotton sheets
a pale tinge lingers where you once lay

eleven weeks in, I missed the sign
five weeks out, you made your point.

*My name is Abi Jolley, I'm 22 years old and I am in my
final year of BA (Hons) English Literature. As well as my
dream of becoming a Secondary English teacher, I aspire
to publish anthologies of autobiographical poetry
covering topics such as illness, travel, romance and
Christianity.*

Wait Here

by Jessica Green

Wait here.
Here,
In the exact place to which
You
Began to understand that you
May
Drop me upon my skull and
Never
Realise the severity and how I
Understand
That you will never know
How
My head is hurt and the cut is
Small
But it's there and all I can think is that
I
Can no longer cope as I
Truly
Love you so painfully but I
Am
Just there, bruised and dead.

By Jessica Green, Fashion and Dress History, UOB.

Leaving Omtepe

by Chris Sciacca

It's not about the birds and bees anymore, it's bees and
frogs. Death magic.
A worldwide vanishing act set in motion. A slow-swirl
wake in place of still water.
As the ship shrinks the shore, the volcano phallus looms,
an obvious fallacy
Of causality. They say the Chinese appetite equated bull
sharks with erections
And so too marked their decline, the beaches now a
paradise of finless calm.

On the upper deck, a fever of five suns. A man forks
through shredded chicken
In a ceramic bowl. A tourist jabs a straw into a young
coconut and drains it dry.
Chalchiuhtlicue yawns, the waves a gentle cradle. The
captain lowers the brim
Of his weathered hat, eavesdrops the old deck hands
mulling the latest rumors
As if sharing swigs of spiced rum, unreserved, their spirit
suddenly evaporating.

In the dead altitude of night, two lost hikers, baited
downward by glimmering
Flecks of village light, walked straight off a cliff. Weeks
until the kettle of vultures,
A beacon of a different feather, aided their recovery.
Nature's precision but Time's
Parallax. The odds of being in the wrong place at the
wrong time yet not missing
The boat. A ferry still offering, unmoored and idling. A
wisp of diesel thinned to sky.

Jellywasps!

by James Novis

The Bumblefish buzzled from a crevice,
Of the coral coated hive,
Seeking cauilflower nectar to store in the Caulicomb,
But the Jellywasps!
The Jellywasps!
The nasty, sticky Jellywasps!
Hovered, lurking, skulking, scheming,
Around the bumble home.

The vexatious vespas verbalified,
Their intentions far from fair,
A sickly, spiccato, whispy-hiss played on vibraphone,
"The Bumblefish!
The Bumblefish!
The dozy, helpless Bumblefish!
We'll steal his stripes, his precious stripes,
And wear them as our own."

The Bumblefish was amboozled roughly,
By the coral coated hive,
Stripped of his gold'n'black striped scales by vile jelly foes,
The Jellywasps!
The Jellywasps!,
The vile, tricksy, Jellywasps!
Triumphantly rejoicing in
The poor Bumblefish's woes.

The Bumblefish knock-shocked and shuverring,
Regained his cool composure,
And hammered with all six fins on the coral covered door,
The Bumblefish!
The Bumblefish!
The clever, plucky Bumblefish!
Alerted Guardy-Ants to rid,

Jellywasps for evermore.

The Bumblefish retriebled his thieved pelt,
And snuck safe into the hive,
Leaving Guardy-Ants to shatterize wicked waspish bone,
The Jellywasps!
The Jellywasps!
The broken, beaten Jellywasps!
They'll never come a-calling,
And'll leave the Bumblefish alone.

James Novis is a second year student, studying to teach English in secondary school, at the University of Brighton.

Shadows

by Clare Brown

What happened to that little girl with a smile so
sweet
that butterflies sprang in delight?
She sits there and moans; bitter and twisted
in a room without light.

They say the past is gone but her father beat his old
fashioned ignorance into her,
shaped her with shadows long forgotten,
and his demons live on.

I wish you would break the tension, shake free
out of the cocoon and be released
into a future that's all yours. Flutter your wings and
fly
little sister, flutter your wings and fly.

*Recently completed the introduction to creative writing
course at the University of Brighton and has performed
her poems at various events including the Poetry Cafe in
London, York Lesbian Arts Festival and at Brighton Pride
in the literature tent.*

1994

by Georgia Betts

1994.

A hand on bare flesh. A flutter beneath the surface. Fresh paint impregnated my nostrils and sent a shiver of excitement down my spine. Flat-pack furniture boxes were leaning against the hallway wall awaiting your arrival. The newly decorated room was small. A box room really. However, I figured that you wouldn't mind, and by the time you did, I'd be able to give you the world. A party for you had been thrown the day before, and I couldn't see the scuffed and stained carpet for the amount of presents you had been showered with, which was both a blessing and a curse. I found myself tripping over generic cuddly toys (including Baby), a silver photo frame which is on your windowsill now, the tiniest pair of socks I have ever seen (they still managed to drown your feet a few months later) amongst a number of practical gifts I had no idea how to use, and whose bright colours and fancy names intimidated me. You began to feel real. My daughter. My world.

2001.

A bright blue school uniform hung in your wardrobe. It stood out because almost everything else was pink. Your room was now a fair size, with a window looking over our garden which was littered with your things. A small trampoline took pride of place on the grass, and often dumped next to it was your Barbie bike, which had a bright pink frame and sparkly silver and pink tassels on each handlebar. Your favourite. The silver photo frame sat on your chest of drawers, with a picture of you on your first birthday, sat on my lap with a grin on your face accompanied by a handful of chocolate cake. Your carpet was a soft, cream masterpiece that was smothered by an abundance of Barbie dolls, colouring books, crayons, Disney story books, videos and the contents of your dressing up kit. I remember Christmas Day of 2000, when you threw a tantrum until myself and your mother allowed you to wear your brand new princess costume all day. Mum was furious when I said yes after she'd bought you a special outfit with matching hair bands for that day, but I could never say no to my little girl.

2008.

You wore a tie to school at 14. It was on the floor of your bedroom along with the rest of your uniform··· and your wardrobe. Pink had been deemed 'un-cool' upon starting a new school and so you set me to the task of redecorating. Green was your new ideal. Apparently, green was indicative of 'sophisticated'. Anything for you. Makeup stained the cream carpet I'd laid down almost 10 years before, and I spent my weekends scrubbing carpet cleaner into the floor. Posters of boys from bands and TV were plastered over your walls, along with photographs of your friends. The silver photo frame had been moved to your bedside table to make room for your makeup and jewellery and hairdryer and whatever else was deemed as necessary for you to function. You bought your first pair of high heels. The same feeling of intimidation from before you were born returned.

2013.

You have a brand new room. It is not dissimilar to the size of your first room. It has a bed and a desk and a wardrobe and a chest of drawers. The curtains are

decorated with garish colours and ugly patterns and I can feel you and your mother squirming at them before either of you comment on them. You'll soon have decorated your new room with photos of us and your friends, good luck letters and your perfumes and the fairy lights your sister bought you to make you feel cosy in your new room, and you'll forget all about the distasteful curtains. You've moved to university and I'm so proud. My baby girl, becoming an adult. No more fancy dress costumes or Barbie dolls on the floor, no bike carelessly discarded in the back garden by a small blonde mess who had been promised an ice lolly. Your new room looks out onto a field. It will be filled with brand new memories of a brand new life you have to set out for yourself. Your new carpet is also not dissimilar from the stained and scuffed carpet of your first home, keeping the secrets of those who had begun their new journeys years before you. My world is small, yours is growing, and as you place your worldly belongings into this little room, my world gets smaller. You get out the silver photo frame of me and you, the one with the cake smeared all over your face, and place it on your windowsill. "Love you dad".
I love you too, baby girl.
Dad.

I Lost My Hair in Heidelberg

by Michael Dunn

I lost my hair in Heidelberg
I'm an ice-cream salesman and she
Asked for all the toppings
I gave her the aftermath, but only
Before we went shopping
I'm a magician who lives by the bar
I settle sleazy deals and I only ever ask for more
When suddenly, I feel the need to take life in hand
And wild nights lie wakeless under the strand
A cutthroat in a heart of diamonds,
Coarsely grinding ash
Into something so pure, yet crass
I'm a gentleman. And a genuine man
But when dealing out the cards
I'll deal you my left hand.

*The dandy poet from a small village in a corner of Kent
fuses folk, blues and prog to the background of lyrics he
has transformed from poems about love, desire and
escapism. The scattered mind of Michael Dunn, who
employs the apt moniker Drunken Poets Society, often
steps on stage with just himself and his guitar to create
an acoustic atmosphere that connect his music to the
crowd.*

Window Watching

by Alice Wadsworth

Stung eyes watch four red balloons retreat across the sky, flashing off a stray ray of light, hiding out of reach behind the pane. Effervescing, rapidly: xylophone voices float up from the street. Each strained screech fights for dominance as they rise into the anonymous atmosphere and discordantly harmonize with the traditional wailing siren. Thrown together they entwine like rising smoke, and dance over the rooftops out of view.

Heavy, lying structures cut the brick blocks up, creating rivulets, standing stoically, imposing order for idle wanderers: the city drags itself back from the sea.

A stern man's voice ricochets around the children's, hesitating with uncertain fear, drawing them along. Suppose he sees another man, with a look he reluctantly recognizes, or perhaps a flaccid wool hat lies hung on a railing, small enough to unnerve contaminated eyes.

Here is the city.

Pitter patter pinches the pavement, pirouetting back into itself indefinitely. The voices dim, and then drown. Fading red brick, punctuated by warped, doubled, self-reflective, windows. Standing firm: their faces turned to the sea. As glitter catches the eye in separate and random stabs, warm yellow holes begin to punctuate the undulating grid of blocks, catching here, and there, a flash, an eye. Faces lean flat with windows, back against the rain, leaning back, back to the sea.

Here is the light.

Cold rain on plastic wrappers clinks like knives on forks. Gaudy, useless, wrappers drift, blown by furies, guided by bricks; searching for dark corners. Somewhere to sleep. First we hide our waste, then we build a maze, and it hides itself. Discarded, empty, packets can't see the levels, the intuitive rules, but try earnestly in self-aware isolation. Fury stomps through the grid, wreaking havoc where it is allotted: she marks her domain by default. All voices are drowned out in the rain, the storm, the children's babble silenced. Why fear the rain, the storm. I blame the rain for the city, for my fear: sustaining itself and making me this way.

Here is the city; here comes the rain.

Here comes the rain; here is the city.

Here am I.

My warped window gives no yellow glow. Just out of life's focus. Layers stand insolently between the rain and I, stemming us as we flow, creating new routes out of old restrictions; new points at which to divide ourselves and spread. To each drop its path; spreading out, drawing in. They pool at street level, and run towards the retreating sea.

No longer am I another child floating on a babbling balloon.

I am still spread across the pane, across the city. Nerves trace their paths over the cold, transparent surface: Nerves trace their path under the cold, translucent city.

Today, I have no excuse.

In the city is reflected my bed, running red. Half in front, half behind.

The rules and levels are clearer, while my head feels muggy.

Here comes the rain; here is the city.
Here am I.

Alice Louise Wadsworth is an English Literature student in her final year of her degree. She has written for several online publications, and some print, on the subject of music, politics, art, fashion and feminism. This is her first submitted work of short fiction, preferring previously to keep it all in a slowly disintegrating chest of drawers, so as to avoid embarrassment and intimacy. This piece is dedicated to Pauline Coonan, for her inspirational strength, without which the chest of drawers would never have been opened.

Kodak Revelation

by Allie Rogers

I am holding up slides to the light. And there isn't much
really. December afternoon ebbing away and grubby strip
lights struggling – flickering and humming overhead. I'm
only doing it because it's raining.

My plan had been to walk up the river. Walking up rivers is
good when you feel lost. The river has purpose. And this
one, with its broad tidal estuary, always seems more
determined than most. But the rain soaked through the
shoulders of my coat in the five minute walk from the
station to this flea market. I couldn't stand the wet feet, the
rising chill in my body. So I'm skulking. I'm waiting, with no
intention of parting with a penny, in this big old barn
stuffed with ancient garden rollers, wicker chairs, bits of
crockery in glass cases, old Blue Peter annuals. The
woman at the desk has clearly recognised me as a
hopeless case and gone back to her coffee and magazine.

Boxes of slides are even better than old photographs,
aren't they? The miniature mountains and steam trains, the
specks of family dogs clutched against tiny girls in anoraks,
they are made more precious by the format of the image.
Rigid cardboard frames on a shrunken world. You could fill
your pockets with them and be rich as Croesus on other
people's lives.

There's a set here – I keep coming upon the same bay from
different angles. There's a woman with a ponytail and a
child on her hip – standing to the left or the right of the
sweep of view, sometimes. I can imagine the man waving
her this way and that, shouting out instructions. Then here
they are on the steps of a B&B – closer this time – and I
can really see her face. And she's you.

I mean, she can't be you. Of course she can't be you. These slides are forty years old. But there she is, headscarf and little mac belted at her waist, knee-high boots, and your face – smiling. So, what? Maybe she's your mum. Maybe that little kid, always turned away to look at the sea, maybe that's you.

I put the slide aside and start sifting in earnest, picking out every Kodak yellow square. I hold them up – next, next, next – looking at his obsession with the bay, the arc of water and the sand rim, the British summer skies. Wales? Cornwall? The story is running in my head – fast. Maybe these are long-lost slides of a summer holiday when your wobbly tooth came out in a toffee apple. Maybe, in a minute, there'll be one of you close-up – proud by a sandcastle with a lolly stick flagpole. Or you on a donkey – brave in a stripy sun hat. Maybe he threw them all away, your Dad, because something happened that summer. Maybe I'm being gifted this whole story as some sort of explanation. Or maybe it's just some small consolation from God because I can't have you.

There are 18 slides. None has a better image of the woman and child than the one on the steps of the B&B. I take it over to an Art Deco lamp – green glass glowing like the egg of some magic bird. Please. I tilt the lamp and the image floods with light. The woman is nothing like you. The child is just a child.

I stack the little squares together in the corner of the box. It's stopped raining so I head for the river.

Allie Rogers is a Brighton-based writer of short stories and flash fiction. She has had work published in the Yellow Room Magazine. Her flash fiction piece 'Cool for Cats' was published in the Salt Anthology of New Writing 2013 as she was a runner up in the Salt Flash Fiction Competition of that year. She blogs some of her work at http://allierogers.wordpress.com/

The Home of Myself

by Argyri Chrysanidou

In my head inhabit voices. I hear them all the time. One of them is my best friend. We are quite similar and opposite at the same time. Another one is just somebody that I used to know. I know she's there, I even hear her, but act as if I'm better. The most distinct one is my eternal enemy. We get on very well but despise each other. The rest of the voices are like chess pawns. They are black, they are white, they eat up each other and make vicious plans against everyone and themselves. I am telling you, it is a whole world of voices in my head.

Lyca, my best friend, was weirdly in a good mood yesterday. I could hear her sing happy songs about bloomy Mondays into my ear, so I decided to get out of the bed with eyes half shut as the midday sun was blinding me. She said she was happy for the winter sun, as because of me she had not felt its warmth in her voice in quite a long time; since I had last seen it.

When Matilda woke up in my head, I pretended like she was not there. She started narrating a story from my childhood; something about wolves, and little girls, and little girls eating wolves. It had been a long time since I last paid any attention to her. My mom said she was the one giving me the weird dreams. I did not mind my dreams, though. They gave me yet another choice of a world to live. I often think I am trapped in this material world. I often think I could turn into a fairy and sneak into material people's dreams. I would turn into whatever I wanted there; I would be a black African woman with my baby tied tightly on my back; I would be the girl who gave up everything and got lost, never to be found by 'her own' people again, lost on a beach in Grenada; I would be a slimy little caterpillar, brown and hairy, and I would turn into a gigantic butterfly and die; I would be a magical water spring, playing with the passers-by wishes. I would make them all come true and watch the world regret their greed.

Nyla had always been my favourite name, until she turned up in my head. Her tone is hoarse and lovely. She always talks to me about flying. I hate her. I know she is always waiting to drown my happiness.

After a warm shower I put on my clothes and decided to take the dog out for a walk. Ira ran towards me as I entered the garden and jumped on me in ecstasy. They say dogs apparently feel the same way when they see their owner as humans when they are in love. I appreciate it as I tend to have really friendly feelings towards this dog, even though she sometimes bites.

Matilda started talking to Lyca about a long-forgotten love of hers. Her lover was a gentle, feminine voice who gave me comfort. Her name was Sarah and she was kind and loving. She was my shelter when the rest of the voices shrieked in my head. For a moment I forgot about her as Ira was trying to chew a used tissue she found on the ground. This dog eats everything, even stones. Apart from the leash around her neck, she is free; a free spirit who eats stones.

Sarah had to go, mother said. I defended her, I fought for her. She had to go. Such a loss of me.

47

I was near the forest by then and admired Ira's shiny black hair. The leash did not seem to make her unhappy, but I think she just didn't know better. I decided to free her. She didn't think about it twice, she gave a jump and ran away, deep into the forest.

I locked myself up in my room for the rest of the day. My mother was worried sick for the dog and went out looking for her. She said that Ira was raised to be a house dog and did not know how to survive on her own, much like myself.

Ira turned up this morning. I was already awake as Nyla kept whispering things to me the whole night. She sneaked into the garden, holding something in her little cute jaws. She looked at me looking at her through my window and dropped the carcass on the freshly cut grass. She pushed it with her puppy head towards me and looked again. She turned around and happily walked away making little jumps.

I went outside and looked at Ira's gift to me. It was a dead bird.

Lyca, Nyla and Matilda were arguing over what I should do just a little earlier. I thought I wanted to grow wings and fly, and find Ira, and if nature wanted so, be her prey.

My life has been the loss of me; all the voices in the world could never possibly replace mine. I have been told I am meant to stay, my body and mind want me to be elsewhere, though. So I take my white nightgown and go.

One Time Eating a Mushroom

by Austin Macfadden

See, sometimes it's funny the things you forget. It's sometimes the things you told yourself that you were always going to remember. My older brother Mike remembers this one time— he's also the one is who is good with the dates—I was helping my Mom outside in the yard. She was doing gardening or something, and our dog Rita was running around our garden's trapezoidal shape. See, my Mom didn't really like Rita and was always annoyed with the fact that Rita, use to shit in the house. It was in April or the Summer. Mike says he was putting all of the rocks in a line through the yard, while my mother did the weeding; her knee bent on a foam pink flower that was dirty on the bottom. He remembers that I just had my arm outstretched, holding something between my fingers. He says I was four and had on a hat. He kept putting rocks in a line and Mom came over to look at what I was holding. This turned out to be a mushroom—he says it must have been something you just find around in the yard. The mushroom itself: had a pale, fading white cap with dark damp weaves and folds underneath. He says that worse yet, this one was a bit bigger than some of the others he'd seen and had a small mouth bite out of it; the last remnants of which I swallowed as Mom recognized this. 'I ate a mushroom,' was what I was saying and held it out before dropping it. Mom, had her contacts out for the yard work, and at first, saw her youngest child, hand out and chew on something. For a split-second in she must not have thought anything of it; must have been a snack—like

49

all of the food she had taken take to airports, backseats, restaurants and theaters. Mike says that he kept putting the rocks in a line, Mom lowering her facing not-even-starting to identify what it was, I had been holding. He remembers that Rita stopped barking for a minute and everything was silent.

'I ate a mushroom.' I said.

'What, what was that sweetie?'

Mike says that he only remembers thinking that he should stop moving the rocks, so he did and it looked like Mom was going to explode. He says that it was only when Mom rushed over to me, grabs my wrist, and it was, then, that I started crying. I had just been holding out, what looked to be the single most important thing in the universe, until I showed everybody what it was.

"AAAAAAHHHHHH!' she calls out.

"My son ate this!" She yells and Rita starts barking again. Mom ran into the house and ran back, holding a small brown bottle. He remembers her pouring some of its liquid onto a little spoon and pushing it in my mouth. She went inside and told Mike that she was going to call Poison Control.

She stood on the back steps with a phone pressed to her ear, saying, "My son ate a mushroom! – Yes, yes, of course I gave him some Ipecac—" That's when Mike says I vomited on the mushroom and the grass.

Mom put the phone down on her shoulder for a second. Kind of breathed a sigh of relief.

And Rita went over there and ate-up the puke.

Austin likes writing and various other things. He can't remember if he's ever been in an ambulance or not.

Biochemistry

by Beth Lowesmith

Dopamine butterflies announce themselves within,
and we celebrate- reactions manifesting,
Oh how I thrive on this insatiable obsession,
Serotonin lights the way of this procession...

Writer. Bibliophile. Wine enthusiast. Ailurophiliac.

Dog Face

by Cathy Watts

You can hear the howling beneath the bridge at Beeding when the tide is right and the moon is full: lost, forsaken, a series of sobs in the liquid darkness.

Beeding Bugle December 24th 2013

Amidst the destruction caused by the ferocious storms experienced all over the country last night, a window to our past was unexpectedly opened which will thrill historians and collectors of folklore alike. It started with a bottle, just one small, glass bottle, discoloured with age but still sealed against the elements. Freed from its riverside grave after many centuries, the bottle rode the floodwaters of the River Arun until it was found by local resident Mrs Fraser out walking with her dog. The bottle itself dates back to the fifteenth century, but yet more exciting is the single piece of parchment it contained. On this was written the compelling tale of "Dog-face" in tiny, but nonetheless legible handwriting. "Dog-face" was an abandoned orphan child who was brought to the Benedictine Priory at Sele in Beeding in 1474. The main part of this extraordinarily powerful story is reproduced for our readers below, adapted into a more modern prose.

··· and the story of the orphan child placed on our doorstep belongs to me, Brother Gilbert, infirmarer at Sele Priory in this year of our Lord 1479. I fear for our future, as the winds of reform are blowing cruelly across the lands. But this tale must be told before I depart and the Priory dissolved.

Our community is small – just five Brethren supervised by Prior Giraud and answerable to the Abbey at Saumur. My tasks are to tend the herb garden and heal the sick, to undo the many ills and mend the wounds that pass through our gates, as well as to supply the herbs we need for cooking and brewing. My garden is most magical in the summer, with its neat rows of raised beds and strong-smelling plants. Applemint for indigestion; tunhoof for the brewhouse; borage for comfort; periwinkle for nosebleeds; comfrey for fractures; the list is endless. The herbs in flower enhance the sensory palette: the silver-blue of the rosemary; the purple-white of the common thyme; the golden-yellow of the lady's bedstraw. My herblore is my life and my livelihood – but enough of me: this is the tale of another soul – a soul lost and tormented.

The child was the first-born son of a local farmer. Much celebration greeted his birth but, very early one morning eight months later, a bundle of what we first thought were rags was placed on our doorstep. It was the boy-child whose body was sturdy, but whose face was troubled by a fine down of dark hair.

The foundling was mine to care for over the ensuing five years that he lived in our small world at Sele Priory. He never spoke – not one word – although his eyes shone with the fire of intelligence. He was christened Firmin by the Brethren meaning 'firm' and 'steadfast' and allowed to sleep in an outhouse of our bakehouse, where he eagerly gathered up the spare rolls and bread when these were offered. Firmin was my silent shadow. He watched closely when I tended my herbs and made up the healing ointments. He sat quietly when, in the evenings, I studied my herblore. Through my guidance he learned his letters and could even write his name in uneven, childish handwriting.

As Firmin grew older, so the down on his face grew more plentiful. I knew that the hair, once cut, would return thicker and fuller, but it had to be removed as, by the time of his second birthday, the hair was noticeable indeed. It covered his forehead, cheeks and chin and gave him the appearance of a long-haired dog-pup. The rest of his body remained smooth and perfect in all its childlike beauty. My first remedy was a spearmint tincture which I applied regularly for several months. Regrettably, it had no effect and the hair persistently drooped over the bright, brown eyes which gleamed beneath its shadow.

Eventually I resorted to scissors as, by this time, Firmin was concealing himself from all visitors, spending his days in isolation. But rumours of the hairy boy-child swept through surrounding villages and the curious would find any pretext to visit the priory to glimpse the 'freak' in our midst. Children were particularly cruel and conceived the nickname "Dog-face" which echoed over the water-meadows as they screamed with laughter at their inventiveness and danced homewards across the fields.

The rumours fanned the fires of prejudice and "Dog-face" was blamed for the poor harvest this summer past. These are days of fear and witchcraft which, along with a general distrust of the Benedictine brotherhood, served Firmin most unhappily. One September night a local mob, garlanded in mistletoe to protect themselves from evil and brandishing farming implements, arrived at our gates. Grain and ale distributed freely dispersed them, but similar incidents followed: rotting offal was piled at our entrance gates whilst blazing, tar-soaked rags were thrown over our protective walls. Eventually higher powers intervened and reforms were mooted. Thus I fear the end of our small world at Sele Priory is nigh and the story of Firmin must be told. For Firmin disappeared one night into torrential rain. Forgotten by most, he is now but a child of five with lengths of abnormal hair on his face and no speech in his mouth. What has become of him I do not know. All searches have failed and I fear for his fate in the hands of others ⋯

Here the story of "Dog-face" ends, as told by your Beeding Bugle. Sele Priory was dissolved in 1480 and the fate of the individual Brethren, as well as "Dog-face" himself, is unknown. But beneath the bridge at Beeding, when the tide is high and the moon is full, a lonely howling can be heard quite distinctly – if you listen carefully.

Cathy Watts teaches languages in the School of Humanities. She has written four books for children based around the seashore and pondlife (see www.beachhutbooks.co.uk and www.pondlifebooks.co.uk) and is currently writing primary school languages books with Routledge.

Like Father Like Son

by Claire Stanfield Owens

Jim pulled himself painfully up out of his armchair then walked slowly to the kitchen to make a cup of tea. He sighed. During his working days as a roofer he'd thought nothing of being up amongst the seagulls on the roofs of Brighton in gales, rain, sleet or snow. Now every joint ached and he had to wrap up in three layers of clothing just to walk down the street in this cold January weather.

Pouring boiling water into his mug, Jim thought about his wife Pam. She had died five years ago. He had been ten years older than her, and always thought he'd go first.

Two teaspoons of sugar stirred into the strong, dark tea, and Jim was on his way back to his armchair, watching his step as he carried the scalding cup the small distance across his flat.
He sat down, wearied with the effort and remembered the conversation he'd had with his son Mike the week before. The boy had been moaning about his job: said his boss was exploiting him, not giving him enough time for tea and fag breaks. It was easy to see what was coming. He'd been in this job for about six weeks now, and that was when things usually started to go downhill for Mike. He just wasn't a sticker, and once the novelty of a new job wore off, he was ready to move on.

Mike's last girlfriend, Becca, had been a good one. She was pretty, of course. Mike, a good looking lad,

57

always went for the lookers, but she was sensible too. Jim had reckoned that she might even get Mike to settle down to a job and find a flat together. Becca was a playgroup leader, great with kids, she'd make a wonderful mum. Still, that wasn't going to happen now. Mike had spent New Year's Eve with Becca. It had been a difficult time for her, the first anniversary of her mum's death. They'd had a quiet night in. And what had Mike gone and done the next day? Only dumped her by text. He'd decided she was too boring.

Since then, Mike had been moody and sullen, communicating in grumpy monosyllables, just like he used to as a teenager.

Jim's gnarled hand, gripping the mug of now luke-warm tea, grew limp in his lap, and as he dozed off in his chair, the mug tipped and the tepid brown liquid trickled on to his leg, soaking his trousers.

He woke to a knock on the door, and the sound of the key in the lock followed by footsteps in the tiny hallway.
'Bloody hell, Dad! What sort of a state are you in?' demanded Mike, seeing the dark, wet stain.
'A damn sight better one than you are, 'retorted Jim, embarrassed by the cold damp discomfort of the spilt tea and the ignominy of being found like this. 'I haven't wet myself, son. It's just tea.'
'What do you mean, then, about you being in a better state than me?' asked Mike, aggressively.

'Don't pretend you don't know what I mean. You with your string of tarty girlfriends, your dead-end jobs that last five minutes. When I was your age....'

'Yeah, yeah, you had a steady job, up on the roofs in all weathers, not afraid of a bit of hard graft. I know, I know. But don't tell me you were happily with just one girl all that time. You didn't even meet Mum till you were forty. So, what, were you a virgin till then, or was it all one- night-stands for you?'

Jim was astounded by his son's rudeness, but he felt very old, very tired. Too tired even to be angry.

'Sit down, son,' he said wearily. 'There's something I want to say.'

Mike came, grudgingly, to sit opposite his father.
'Look', said Jim, 'I know you think I'm just some boring old codger who hasn't got a clue. Well, maybe I am, but I was young once. Meeting your mum was the best thing that ever happened to me, don't get me wrong, but yes, I had a life before Pam, and I made some pretty big mistakes. I don't want you to do the same.'

'Go on then, tell me,' Mike said gruffly.
'Well, I had an eye for a pretty girl, just like you do, and there was one in particular, Sylvia. Absolutely gorgeous she was, long blonde hair, smile that lit up the room.'

Jim smiled wistfully.

'We weren't much older than you are now, and we were close, really close. Anyway, she got pregnant. She wanted to keep the baby and get married, but I was scared – terrified – and talked her into getting an abortion.'

'Anyway, eventually we split up on really bad terms. Friends told me how cut up Sylvia was, and I was wretched too. I even hit the bottle for a while, but I was too proud to go back to her, to tell her I was sorry, to tell her I loved her. As time passed, it got better, and I met your mum.'

'Did mum know about her and the – the – thing?'
'Nope,' Jim paused.
Mike looked thoughtful, and marginally less sullen.
'So now do you see why it upsets me so much that when you finally meet a truly good woman, Becca, you throw your chances away. Don't be the fool I was. You should seize the chance while you can. There. I've said it.'

'Dad, I've already done it. If you hadn't gone off on one the minute I walked through the door, I'd have told you. Becca's got a flat, I'm moving in with her this weekend.'

'Come here, son' Jim said, standing up stiffly and holding out his arms.

Father and son hugged for the first time since Pam's funeral.

'Come on Dad, let's get you into some dry trousers,'
Mike said.

*We moved to Brighton in 2011, and I'm now a 'mature'
part-time student on the MA TESOL course at the
University of Brighton. I'm a member of an informal
writing group, and we get together whenever we can to
support each other in our work.*

Uni2

by Dave Simpson

Executive Vice Chancellor Leyla King walked towards the three hundred metre long curved atrium which stood at the centre of Uni2. It was 9.23 on the first day of term.

She looked up at the five storeys of tinted glass, dull steel and matching concrete. They were softened by lush silvery green vegetation which covered the atrium's flat roof and spilled in bunches over the sides of the building. It was a man-made grass, woven together from genetically modified marram grass and strands of razor wire.

'A sense of the human,' Leyla King thought as she studied the sparkling fronds hanging over the front and pointing down the sides of the atrium. Her watch, networked to her admin computer, blinked on as she spoke, 'Contact estates and ask them to schedule a trim for the atrium roof grass.'
'This is being done,' was the instant response.
She continued her walk through soft autumn air towards the quietness of an almost empty building.
'First assignments and matched answers are now on-line,' said her admin computer. 'And the pass rate was approved by finance five minutes ago. We are in advance of our competitors.'
'Put a selection of the congratulatory email to staff on screen,' she said. 'I'd like to individualise a comment to the colleague responsible.'
'There are three generic praise statements which match the tier of academic responsible.'

'Fine; I'll choose one of them when I reach my desk.'

She looked around as she approached the atrium's entrance. 'This is the institution's heartbeat,' she said to herself. A pair of double doors slid back. Their hiss was a breath of comfort for Leyla King. This was her moment; procedure, policy and practice inter-locked through a familiar voice which said, 'Welcome to Uni2. You are now approaching the atrium.'

She breathed in deeply.

'Have you swiped your UniCard?'

She ran her card through a swipe machine just inside the doors. Her image appeared on a screen facing her.

'We will now match your card image with our records. This may take a few seconds.'

Her image flickered for a moment until a second one from the Uni2 data base blended over her card image feature by feature until the voice said, 'Please take your card and all your items with you. Doors opening.'

She walked towards a second, inner set of doors which opened noiselessly. A metal turnstile clicked electronically as she approached. The same voice spoke again, 'There is some irregular pulsing from the battery of your seventh tier management chip. Would you like me to book an off-peak low rate visit to the Medicentre?'

'No, that is not necessary.'

'The Medicentre is offering a free service or exchange for a limited period, with a special discount for Uni2 card holders.'

'No thank you.'

'We are offering double Uni2 points.'

'No thank you.'

'Have you brought your own bags today? If you have would you like a student ambassador to carry them to your office for you?'

'No thank you.'

'Now please step forward. Remove all books for approval by placing them on the scanner to your right.'

She felt her watch start to vibrate as the voice continued with, 'You have 17 emails and all your books are authorised.'

The turnstile clicked again, 'Thank you for choosing entrance seven. I am sponsored by Power Learn, a natural cognitive accelerant which is a gateway to efficient learning.'

She stepped through into the atrium's main concourse to be met by a welcoming coffee-like aroma floating towards her and a bulky figure wearing a fluorescent high visibility jacket edged in dark blue and purple.

Beyond the windows fronds and stems of the marram grass wire bent awkwardly in the breeze.

'Good morning Vice Chancellor,' said Ray Light, the floor manager for the Concourse. Her unhurried strides took her to the atrium's centre where she paused to breathe in the gently circulating scented air, noticing how it always seemed fresher early in the morning before the computer systems switched fully over from store to serve and staff woke in their 24 hour office dorm pods. Add in students coming in from the rented by the day campus aparthotel and it could all become stale.

'Air quality?'

'We'll bring cinnamon and apple on stream within the next half hour because that's when demographic data suggests academic staff will want breakfast,' said Ray Light. 'The new scent will make them buy a coffee and a pastry.'

'Revenue implications?'

'Average spend will be up six per cent which is in line with the growth target in our action plan.'

'Good,' she said.

'The lights are working properly?'

'Yes we've put in an aroma feed into every twelfth one. We've managed to equalise the intensity so that it is distributed evenly across the ground floor.' He knew that the focussed use of aroma therapy was a cornerstone of her sustainability initiatives designed to upgrade the Uni2 environmental policy.

'And if there are large crowds this morning for the distribution of pre-owned assignments?' she asked.

'We'll use one of our cocoa activators.'

'A bedtime drink?' she asked. 'I thought some students fell asleep and tried to pull the curtains only to find that they were stainless steel fire shutters.'

'Cocoa always does the trick,' he said. 'Conjures up comforting images of teddy bears, bedtime stories, slows everyone down.'

'Control the atmosphere,' she thought, 'and you control learning. Control learning and you control income.'

She continued towards the lifts.

Stability.

9.32.

The Black Plate

by Dan Chapman

The reader may recall a short story by Borges, the principle concern of which was, loosely, cartography, and in particular the complications the notion of accuracy presents to the map-maker. Perfection is the inexhaustible object of our time, perhaps of any time. When faced by a sea of shadows, however, and with the ardent purpose of exploration, one is wise to be guided by a map. It was just such a premise that drove the work of Dr. Arthur Bransby forward, a life's work that would culminate in his settling nearby to the East Sussex village of Rye.

At first, the arrival of the clever doctor, and his handsome wife, had attracted considerable interest. As time had gone on, however, interest in a man who showed little interest in others was soon to subside, and after a few years it was all but forgotten that Dr. Bransby and his wife inhabited that picturesque little cottage at all.

What was remarkable about Dr. Bransby, besides his considerable intellect, was that he had almost succeeded, after a time approaching nearly thirty years, in completing the map that he had set out to draw. It would not be remarkable, perhaps, if it were not for the extraordinary nature of what the map charted, for in essence what the map charted was nature itself. Bransby had undertaken a project almost inexplicable to his fellow professionals. A project that, in map-making terms, might be something analogous to the charting of the entire universe. In spatial terms, Bransby's subject was nowhere near as vast, but in attempting to chart the internal workings of the human brain, Bransby's subject extended far beyond three dimensions. He sought more than the orientation of the organ, Bransby wanted to travel deeper into the mind than anyone had previously thought possible. Thought itself was the territory. Therein, for Bransby, lay a crucial separation, much like that of body and soul.

So it came to pass that on a dreary and drizzly November evening he eventually beheld the accomplishment of his toil. It lay before him in fragments that only he understood. Muriel was away, and only the dog that lay sleeping, like the fretted Gothic steeple of the church seven miles distant, was there to share with him in his glory. Like the cartographers of that Borgian Empire, however, Bransby's conquest was not without its limitations. For it would soon dawn on him that there was still but a tiny shadow within his mind that seemed to develop almost as soon as the map was completed. There was within his map, then, a small 'Mount Richard', which he had not consciously put there himself.

He asked Lutwidge, who stirred on the sofa, "Where's that? Is that not a clear description?"

The dog was too lazy to reply, perhaps, and outside a storm was beginning to set in. As the rain started to lash at the panes as if they were defiant sailors, Bransby rose and walked out to the kitchen. He muttered to himself, "I have no other name for it, it is the area where the pots and pans and ovens are."

In Muriel's absence the kitchen was never tidy, and the washing up rarely done, so with Lutwidge sleeping still on the sofa, Bransby set to work in clearing the pots and pans that had gathered there. It took Bransby around half an hour to clear the kitchen, and he remembered happily the days they once had been able to afford help for such tasks.

Outside, the storm had grown steadily worse. Lutwidge noticed this, and came into the kitchen to warn his master. As he did so, the electricity failed, and Bransby was left to dry up by candlelight. Lutwidge sat loyally by him as he did so.

The time was ten as Bransby reached the final plate, a black one. At first he thought that he was mistaken, tiredness perhaps, or the low light, but as he went to put it away in the cupboard he noticed a smear, about an inch or so in diameter. He rubbed at the plate with the dishcloth again, and was sure he had cleared it, but upon returning it to the cupboard noticed the mark once more. He took it out again to look more closely. Lutwidge sniffed at the plate and whimpered, while lightning and thunder crashed concurrently outside.

The lightning revealed to Bransby that the smear was indeed there, it was not a trick of the eye or of the light. He rubbed at it again with the dishcloth but it would not go. Reluctantly, he placed the plate back into the cupboard and tried to forget that the mark was there.

That night as he lay awake, with Lutwidge at the end of his bed and sleep far distant, he pondered on the reasons for his alertness. The storm was the visible culprit, but the shadow on the map lay disconcertingly beneath it.

The following morning, as he stirred from a sleep he could not be certain he had actually enjoyed, and stumbled his way downstairs to reconsider his map by daylight, the howling winds still beat the panes and the rain lashed them like a cat o' nine tails. With a pan of water boiling he opened the door and beheld his labour, and was sure his eyes deceived him: it seemed his shadow had enlarged. Unsure, he made toast, and removed the black plate from the cupboard, but of course it was not just the shadow that had grown but the smear too, now covering almost the entirety of the plate.

There are many more details to Bransby's tale, but in the spirit of Borges, just know that in the days that passed, and the many hours of scrubbing at the smear, it simply would not be removed. Instead, it but spread and spread and spread, until it covered not only Bransby's map but everything his map represented, which stayed smeared and shadowed forever after.

Dan Chapman has published 'Looking for Lucy' and 'The Postmodern Malady', both available from Amazon. He studied English and Education and Philosophy and Critical Theory at Brighton between 2007-2011.

The Man Who Had the Hands of a Baboon

by David Chasumba

On one cloudy and wet morning, I woke up to discover that a thief had broken into my grandmother's chicken run and two chickens were missing.

My grandmother, VaSekenhamo, cried out, *'Maiwe! Maiwe!'*

I felt sympathy for her.

'Rwizi, my grandson, go and fetch VaGono, the village headman,' she said when she had wiped away the tears of her wrinkled cheeks.

VaGono was also the 'detective' and witchdoctor of Rugare village.

I watched VaGono, his two aides and Shumba, his dog; meticulously scour through the crime scene. The hinges of the small wooden door of the chicken run were broken. Inside, white feathers were spawn on the wet ground. There was a big, cracked footprint in the wet chicken dung. The other ten chickens in an inner enclosure were untouched.

Shumba, on VaGono's leash, picked the scent of the thief and trailed the movements through the corn fields to Majongwe's homestead. The two aides and I followed close behind VaGono and Shumba.

Majongwe was the notorious village thief. The lanky, middle-aged man with an oval-shaped face and small, darting chameleon eyes lived with his family in an unattractive homestead with four ramshackle huts. The family was shunned by the entire village.

VaGono knocked hard on the door of the

biggest of the four huts. There was a momentary silence.

Then the hut door creaked and swung open. Out came a dreary-eyed Majongwe.

'Good morning. Do you have any knowledge or anything to do with the theft of two chickens from Ambuya Sekenhamo's chicken run last night?' asked VaGono.

'I have nothing to do with that theft,' declared Majongwe yawning.

'Where were you last night?' interrogated VaGono gazing into Majongwe's eyes.

I saw Majongwe's eyes shift away from the gaze of VaGono.

'At home with my family,' replied Majongwe unsure of himself and his hand trembling slightly.

'Can you explain why my dog has picked your scent from the chicken run and trailed it to your home or why we have tracked your big, cracked footprint from the chicken run to here?'

'Pure coincidence, perhaps,' muttered Majongwe confidently.

'We will see about that,' said VaGono unleashing Shumba.

Shumba ran straight through the kitchen hut door and began sniffing animatedly at something wrapped in newspaper in a white dish.

Majongwe's face turned as pale as sick man. 'I couldn't help it. My family was starving,' Majongwe confessed.

'You should pay a fine of three chickens by the end of the month,' ordered VaGono. 'If you fail to pay, I will hand you over to the police.'

A deflated Majongwe nodded his head. We left.

Back at home, I described to Ambuya Sekenhamo the look on Majongwe when he was caught lying. She giggled through her yellow stained teeth.

'Majongwe has the hands of a baboon,' Ambuya Sekenhamo, described him figuratively. 'His hands raided my chicken run like a hungry, baboon raids maize fields.'

I soon learnt that, Majongwe, in his boyhood, had begun stealing the wild fruits that other children had picked and hidden under the soil to hasten their ripeness. In his teens, he graduated to stealing mice from small hunters' mouse traps. In adulthood, he was caught breaking into an old woman's granary and was fined a goat and publicly humiliated.

***

On the following day, when the sun was shining brightly, I saw Majongwe, armed with a bow and arrow, spear and axe and his four dogs passing by the footpath close to our homestead. He disappeared into the dense forest.

'I saw Majongwe going hunting,' I told Ambuya Sekenhamo.

'Since when did Majongwe have hunting prowess?' remarked Ambuya Sekenhamo.

Majongwe returned from his hunting the following day in the sweltering noon sun.

To the surprise of the entire village, Majongwe was trudging on the footpath, heavy laden with the carcass of a big antelope over his shoulder like Jesus bearing the crucifix. His dogs pranced around and wagged their tails.

I gazed until Majongwe had entered his yard and was greeted with claps and ululation by his wife and two teenage children, a boy and a girl.

I admired the hunting prowess of Majongwe that afternoon. But not for long.

VaGono came to our home late in the afternoon hissing like a python. 'Some thief has disturbed the animal trap that I set up in the forest and stolen the animal that had been caught up in it. Who from the village went hunting lately?' quizzed VaGono.

'Rwizi, my teenage grandson, saw Majongwe return from hunting with the carcass of an antelope over his shoulder,' reported Ambuya Sekenhamo.

VaGono, his aides and I rushed to Majongwe's homestead.

In Shona hunting culture, when an animal is caught up in someone's animal trap, you don't steal from the animal trap, lest an evil spell is cast on you. This has been a hunting custom for many generations.

Upon arrival at Majongwe's homestead, VaGono knocked hard and impatiently on the door of the kitchen hut. There was a momentary silence.

A physically-spent Majongwe emerged from the hut moments later.

'Majongwe, did you disturb my animal trap and steal the game that had been caught up in it?' asked VaGono cutting to the chase.

'I did not disturb your animal trap. I swear,' declared Majongwe.

'Alright, then. Only a fool steals from a village witchdoctor,' said VaGono leading the way out of Majongwe's homestead.

***

I was present, as usual, the following morning at VaGono's court, when Majongwe publicly confessed and asked forgiveness for stealing the antelope from VaGono's animal trap.

When Majongwe and his family ate the meat of the antelope for supper the previous night their abdomens began to swell and swell like they were pregnant.

VaGono felt deep sympathy for Majongwe and his family. He mixed his traditional herbs and gave them to drink. Immediately, the swelling of their abdomens went down. Majongwe swore never to steal anything from Rugare village ever again.

About David Chasumba: I did the Creative Writing: Advancing the Craft short course at Brighton University. My short story, The Promised Land, was published on the Africa Book club website.

Pride and Promiscuity

by Joe Abercrombie

Mascara never

stained her cheeks

her lip gloss

was always

smudged

Shoes, booze

and

men with tattoos

are all

she'll ever

love.

Joe Abercrombie is twenty three, currently living and studying in Brighton'

Excerpt from Waldeinsamkeit

by Ellie Exton

The third plum was perfect. Where the others were hard and yellow sour within, the third was dark with almost-ruin, the colour we mean when we say plum. The skin fell away from the flesh as Ana bit, and its juice sweetly trickled over her wrist and chin. Ana's body sang; she felt light, buoyed up by a surging wave –

'You ought to wash those before you eat them.'

Ana spat the stone and wiped her fingers on the hem of her dress. She turned to her husband, smiling stiffly in an attempt to quell the annoyance she felt.

'I'm sure it won't do me any harm.' Lifting the potful of fruit, she twisted her features into a scowl – snatching up the heavy pot had irritated her sciatic nerve, and a hot shard of pain pierced her body from the back of her hip to her knee. She took them as far as the kitchen door and set them down by Teddy's feet, looking up at him.

'What's wrong?' He sounded exasperated, amused.

'Nothing. Hey, we can't eat all of these. They'll go bad.' There had been a glut, and though she had filled a large casserole dish to the brim, there were still some left on the tree.

'Maybe you could make jam out of them.'

'Mm, that would be nice. I'm not sure I know how to make jam,' she lied. 'Could you have a go?'

Teddy laughed, '– of course not.' He bent and took the plums into the kitchen. 'Haven't you got a recipe somewhere?' he called.

'I expect there's one in Delia,' Ana replied, sitting on the back step and starting to work her feet out of her walking boots. 'I made chutney last year in the autumn; I expect it's the same sort of process. Could you set the bath running? My back is – '

'Cheerio love. I'll see you tomorrow night. Don't bother yourself with dinner; I won't be back until late.' Teddy's voice came from down the hall. Ana craned her neck to see him buttoning his coat.

'Tomorrow night? You never said anything about⋯ where will you be?'

'It's the away day – I told you weeks ago!'

'Well it's no good unless you remind me,' Ana began, but found herself speaking to an empty house as the front door clicked to.

There were bed-sheets hanging from a line next door, folded over in two. As a particularly strong wind passed, the sheets filled with air with a muffled crash like a swollen wave rolling into a wall of rock. The sheets deflated with a sea-spray sighing.

When Ana was ten years old, her womanhood had torn its way out of her child's body, leaving a patina of puckered, livid lines across her breasts; hips; buttocks; her round, firm upper arms; her thighs – almost every place that made her a woman, but for her stomach. Settled in the bath, one curled knuckle pressed into the sore point of her back, Ana gazed across the peaks and vales of her body at the rows of scars. They reminded her of a field – a piece of fallow ground, ploughed but never planted. From the plastic dollies and miniature prams onwards, almost from the time she herself was born, life had cut her out in the shape of a mother. Yet her blood still came once a month, a violent reminder of her failure. She could remember the first time she walked to school after she started her period, unused to the discomfort of a sanitary towel. It felt like a nappy – cumbersome and conspicuous. Hot shame darkened her face and prickled under her arms; she felt sure that everyone could see.

The palms of Ana's hands had been roughened by the regular handling of her spade and hoe, and her fingernails were frayed, short, and darkened with embedded soil. In bed, Teddy would often clasp them, laughing, and complain that he felt as though he were sleeping with a manual labourer. Well – he was. But, 'you know – a bloke.' There had been a time when he adored her body. He had decided to keep it, tried to learn it by rote, but he'd long since lost interest. It had let them both down.

Ana placed her hand on her hip – childbearing hips, her mother had called them – bending her wrist to fit the dip of her waist, where the heel of her palm met with an unfamiliar lump. Had she been bitten? She twisted her body to look at it, her breath hissing between her teeth as the movement made her back twinge again. The small, raised mark was not itchy, but a little painful, and looked strangely dark under the skin. Ana eased herself out of the now lukewarm water and, after delving into the cabinet above the sink, rubbed calendula balm into her side. She wrapped herself in a large terrycloth bathrobe and made it only as far as the upstairs landing before her footsteps faltered and she stood gazing absently at a smudge on the wall, carelessly dripping. Moments later she breathed in deeply, roused herself, began to pad down the stairs with one knee creaking and carpet fluff sticking uncomfortably to the bare soles of her feet. At the foot of the stairs she wavered, stopped again.

Sometimes a crisp white collar; the smell of rich, moist earth; a breath of icy sea spray or some other little thing – a ripe plum – will elevate a person to a state of absolute, almost painful peace. It was one of Ana's dearest wishes that in a moment of exquisite beauty such as this she should be struck dead without knowing a thing about it. Nothing frightened her more than the thought that one day she might eat her dinner in front of the television, brush her teeth, piss, undress for bed, read a chapter of her book, then go to sleep and simply come to an end.

Small Town Boy

by Cyd Slater

Fuccccckkkkk!!!!

With a start, I awoke from the nightmare, not for the first time, stifling a scream (of which I was now excelling in after all these months) to find the coach was stationary, the engine quiet. At last! I was here! Brighton. The city by the sea, a maritime municipality. The bus was slowly emptying, myriad day trippers animated and raring to go, eager to explore the sights and sounds of this metropolis, politely alighting through the large front access at the front of the Stagecoach.

Gathering my wits, or lack of, the last of the lurid dream fading from my head, I got my muscles working again with a few stretches of my arms and legs, rubbing my neck to get rid of the ache from sitting so immobile on the not-made-for-travelling-too-far seats, ergonomics yet to catch up with the pew designers of mass-roving vehicles. Taking my trusty black, battle-damaged backpack from the shelves overhead I slowly made my way to the door, checking my pocket for my treat at the ending of such a lengthy, coast to coast, journey. Treading off the step onto the concrete of the terminus, stroking my freshly shaven head, glaringly white next to my tanned face, I took in the ambience of the place and saw the prom directly in front of me, taking my doob out of my pocket and, once away from the crowd of the coach station, lighting the white stick with my red (Liverpool!) Clipper, pulling in the reassuring fumes, the feeling of relaxation once again returning to my bones. I once again thought about how life had brought me here, thirty quid in my pocket, a change of clothes in my bag, my diary and Alien Queen safely wrapped in a towel within the holdall. A dream of a new life, a new start, a new me.

Well, here goes, I muttered to myself, smirking, drawing on the thick vapours of my large spliff, the fumes held in my lungs for just long enough to feel the THC enter my bloodstream. I looked up at the cloudless azure sky. It had been a beautiful midsummer all over Britain and continuing in a record breaking heat wave ("Since records began!" the forecasters trumpeted each evening after the news).

The promenade and beach appeared before me as I crossed the dual carriageway that separated the seafront hotels and shops from the shingle strewn seashore. Beautiful, I declared to myself as I pulled on my joint. No sand to be seen. That's a new thing. Certainly wasn't expecting that. A classic Victorian, fairground laden pier to my left and a tumble-down, decaying, dilapidated pier to my right. Shame on the wrecked pier, I mused. I do love strolling out to the sea, not being a swimmer, content to be safe above the waves below.

First things first though. Food! The smoke had got my stomach juices going, a faint rumbling beginning to build as my appetite was awoken.

Looking round, I spied a chipshop. Perfection. Get some stodge in me, get my brain fuelled and let's see where I go. As I walked to the franchised fat fabricator I strolled under a ladder against a wall and glanced at a shop window. 'Room for Rent.

Eastbourne. Call Paul on···' Bonus! Finding a place wasn't taking too long then. My luck was still with me.

Making sure I got a 20p coin in my change from the fish and chips I bought I went back to the shop window and mentally noted down the Eastbourne number, ready to call once I'd filled my empty, marijuana stimulated stomach. Guessing that Eastbourne was a housing estate east of the town centre I smiled to myself that I would soon have a base to launch from.

Finishing the fatty rubbish and screwing the greasy paper into a ball, bin nearby to collect the oleaginous paper, I looked around for an iconic red phone box and prepared myself to make the call. To my disbelief, the voice that answered was Scouse.

–Hi there, Paul Summerville here.

–Hi, I'm just enquiring about the room you have advertised.

–Yes, mate. Can you make it to Eastbourne tomorrow evening?

–Sure. Where is it?

–Just get the no. 12 bus and it's the last stop. Pevensey Road is just off the town centre.

–Thank you mate. See you tomorrow.

And with that I had a room in the bag.

Now to explore this city, the sun slowly setting, the heat of the day gradually fading as my first night in this new place began. To be safe I planned to stay awake through the hours of darkness and snooze when it was busy (therefore safe) and warm on the beach, not the first time I had slept below the stars.

So here I was. New start, new life, blah, blah, blah, et cetera. That first night I wandered aimlessly, taking in the newness of it all, getting my bearings and day—

(or night—)

dreaming of the period ahead. Finding a quiet, secluded spot to put three papers together, I spent the night in a haze. Come what may, I would succeed down here. Every now and then I would find myself on the promenade, deciding to stroll on the pebbles below, resting my feet for a bit, lying on the beach, staring at the innumerable stars overhead, glancing further and further into the distant past of the cosmos, my mind as one with the constellations, floating in the past, wandering into my future. By morning, as the sun rose with a promise of another scorcher, lighting a doob on the empty seashore, I lay down on the cool stones and, finishing the last of my stash, I drifted off into a peaceful, hopeful sleep. But, just before I woke, as expected and almost welcomed, the nightmare made an appearance once again.

Lives of the Poets
by Joe Shier

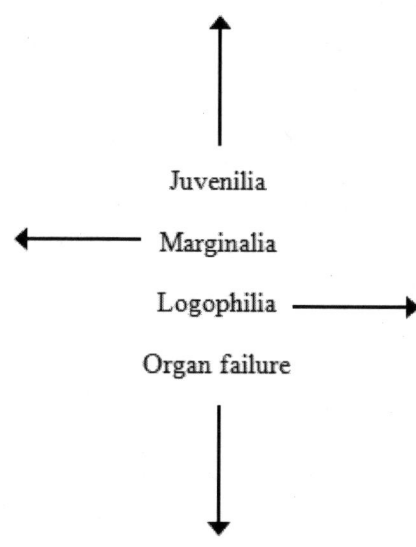

Juvenilia

Marginalia

Logophilia

Organ failure

Joe Shier studied English Literature at the University of Brighton. Now he does as little as possible.

Dear Jude

by Joel Brown

Dear Jude,
Emancipation is over but, still I suffer from society's shackles and chains of hatred. Only in death we are free. I will no longer be black and you will no longer be white. We will have no burdens that weigh heavy on our hearts. As long as I reside in this world, no progress shall be made. I have lost too much. I cannot stray off this path. I disregard any sort of redemption or salvation. Hatred is born in order to protect peace. And with that hatred I shall turn my illusion into a reality. All knowledge gained is baseless. The only truth is this world is darkness. The darkness swallows everything. Even light has shadows. Everybody is filth. I am genuinely sorry. Hope is stronger than fear. With hope, people look to obtain a brighter future that shall ever be out of their grasp while subconsciously accepting the hardships they face. That is why I cannot trust society. That is why I cannot trust man.
Morality does not inherently exist. I still ponder whether I have made the right decision. But, no matter what. Whether you are right or wrong. Whether you love or hate me. Remember I shall always love you. We are just ordinary men seeking justice under the banner of vengeance. You once told me that we could be together, and I hoped for that but, now I see life more clearly. My adolescence molested my innocence. That childhood figure is no more. I camouflage my depression with masquerades of extreme cordiality, courtesy and goodwill towards others. They have no idea. Melancholy seeps through

my eyes. I need to do it. There are no such things as war crimes. War is a crime in itself. The longer they prevail, the more my people suffer. As the time approaches, this is the last time I can write to you. The last time I can express to you. That you are the only person, I have and ever will love.

Till we meet again in the next life...

My name is Joel Brown, an aspiring author who is interested in youth subcultures, gender, race, sexuality and most importantly identity. I see these groups, people and personalities as rebellious flower children who can make any mundane part of existence blossom into their countercultural utopia. You can contact me at joel-br0wn@live.co.uk or J.Brown17@uni.brighton.ac.uk.

Finality

by Ken Clarry

The finality of loneness – small worlds, small words, quiet wars and the *terra incognita* of research.

Everything begins somewhere, but where? Some maintain, some-thing, some-one was, is, there before life began, an incipit being at the origin of existence; the genesis of the spectre of violence? Is it possible to discharge oneself from the spectre or ghost of the feeling that something is absent yet present, invisible but visible? George Steiner seemed to hit the nail on the head when asking – *Is there anything in what we say?* He believed the complex relationship between language and meaning that questions the frailty of truth, what Steiner calls the phoneticlexical-syntactic components of a sentence to meaning, to the semantic whole of that sentence, is out of kilter. He questions the whole concept of what words and language mean and their relationship to each other. Is there anyone there? Is there life before or after death? Can we know of something that logic tells us does not exist?

Language to Steiner materialises as non-sense, words picked, formed at random to mean some 'thing'. The word 'word' could mean or suggest 'war' and the word 'war' could mean 'word'.

What he is getting at is that words, at least in the west, are just words, printer's ink or scratch marks formed into shapes. They do not have any 'pre-established affinity with the objects' they represent, we have bestowed the shape and sound of the word's definition to mean something, but why and how? As we question what words mean, Steiner calls this *a crisis of the word* or war of words, it becomes an abrogation of sense. Like the violence of the *Big Bang*, a collapsing of matter and meaning.

Reading Steiner makes me wonder about another collapsing of matter and meaning, abstract art, and how we might make sense of it all. Artists often have no pre-conceived notion or expectation of what a final work (if there can be such a thing) will be. At times this state resembles 'freefall' where reality flashes past in a blur of non-fixable consciousness. I know, but I do not know. I realise, I feel something but I am unable to define its presence or describe what it is. Terry Eagleton, who like Steiner is a mystic of words, suggests something similar. He wrote that meaning is a kind of constant flickering of presence and absence mixed together. Reading a text is more like tracing this process of constant flickering than it is like counting beads on a necklace. There is also another sense in which we can never quite close our fists over meaning.
When I read a sentence, the meaning of it is always somehow suspended, something deferred or still to come ⋯ and although the sentence may come to an end the process of language itself does not.

Something not dissimilar is going on with the tension between art practice and theory. When we read, an image forms in our head, but the meaning, as Eagleton suggests, is suspended.

Deconstruction as abstract art refuses to recognise absolute meaning; its relationship to 'truth' is fragile. And so an object is suspended, subjected to a type of heterogeneous intensity that exposes its latency and its subjectivity. In the deconstructive paradigm it is the reader who produces the text-image and creates the final piece of the art puzzle. Steiner worries further, what if there was never a starting point, what if everything we think we read and see in texts and in art is pure fiction, made up to while away the centuries? Do we need to imagine 'something', such as Descartes' imperative likelihood of God, in order to escape from the *finality of loneness*? From the sheer tediousness of it all.

The *finality of loneness* has a profound ring to it. Is it possible that artists pick up on some form of chaos frequency, a gabble outside of normal human hearing? If so, artists become reflexive receiving stations tuned to the cultural chatter of the airwaves, to a type of keening.

What I am suggesting is not a kind of spiritualism, although as I write, it begins to look like it.
But if we can hold an idea, a memory in our heads, send, and receive messages and images via satellites, invisibly through a void, anything seems possible. The reference to spiritualism is difficult to shake off, and can be a problem for philosophers and theorists, particularly when dealing with things that are invisible and appear impossible to prove. Art can help: serious painting, music, literature or sculpture, Steiner believes, make palpable to us the unassuaged,

unhoused instability and estrangement of our condition. What he then writes has parallels to what I was thinking about earlier and Eagleton's 'constant flickering of presence and absence'. We are, at key instants, strangers to ourselves, errant at the gates of our own psyche. We knock blindly at the door of turbulence, the non-place of creativity and the *terra incognita* of ourselves.

Steiner is writing about a place well known to artists, a place that although cannot be seen, still exists in an unknown territory (*terra incognita)* of our own mind, being or inner self. We knock blindly, impatiently at the door of our own turbulence; inside there is conflict, confusion, chaos, and a war of words is taking place. Steiner writes of the enclosedness in the texture and phenomenality of the material world, with art alone going some way towards making sense of the sheer inhumanness of matter. It troubled Kant also, who unlike Steiner, thought art ultimately failed to grasp or express the essence of 'truth' that is beyond our known sphere of existence, that is outside our consciousness. We know it is there but we don't know what it is. For Kant, art's failure to encapsulate the absolute essence of Sublimity was its success; its purpose was to act like a signpost. By capturing our attention art demonstrates and invokes the existence of the infinite boundary of existence. It gives hope that there is after all, some-thing, some-one, some-where in the *terra incognita.*

Our World

by Kiefer Holland

Yesterday I moved the furniture,
Put the sofa facing the window –
Its straight back against a strong surface –
I sat, watched, willing the world to slow.

Then I stripped the paper off the walls,
Found it was still concrete underneath,
Sheer grey but faulted, solid but cracked,
Grimacing back at me with bared teeth.

Today I tore away the carpets,
They held tightly to the boards below,
But I was ruthless with their fibres;
They were too soft, they had to go.

Two hours ago I stood back and looked,
Smiled through the salt water on my face
admiring my laborious work.
Took a sledgehammer to the fireplace.

Thirty minutes ago I lay down,
On this cold floor, with my body curled,
As I held tightly on to a ghost,
An apparition, dreams (of our world).

Romeo is Grieving

by Louise Bentinck (Pennington)

If I had been different, if I had not been like I am, perhaps I would not have set out to hurt him in quite the way I did. Even now I find myself conjuring up his face in my mind and feel again that hot coal of jealousy.

I can't duck, sidestep, or out-run it. That's the thing. I lie in bed holding what's left of my Chardonnay and the recollection moves right through me. Yet I still think of him in his conservative blue pyjamas, that scar beneath his brow bone, his hand seeking mine under the bed clothes – memories that peck steadily at my mind.

Part of me is ashamed. I get up and go to the window and stare out into the blackness. I close my eyes willing the images to go way, saying: come on, come on to the dark...

In the distance I hear Romeo calling, his harsh cry growing louder, more insistent. I wonder how long he will keep searching until realisation dawns. A peacock is not supposed to feel deeply and yet it seems to me that Romeo does.

Romeo is grieving.

Louise started writing at an early age and won an award for her short story 'The First Legend'. She has published several times, but also loves writing for performance. Her play, 'Fractured', was performed at Brighton's Little theatre and she has a short film, 'The Left-Hand Path', in post-production.

Small Worlds

by Jessica Moriarty

He emails me from Bolivia to say he made it,

That the air is drier than anything we tasted

In the East where we lived on beer, formaldehyde

And something that even now, feels like love.

In the West he roamed the Inca trail with

An ex model who liked him just the way he is,

Danced shirtless at carnival in warm rain and sequins,

Says the world seems bigger when you travel alone.

He emails me from Bolivia to say he made it

And in the kitchen in suburbia amongst the

Wet wipes and washing and wishes I made for me,

I reach back and tell him – *I always knew you would.*

Jess Moriarty is a senior lecturer in Creative Writing at the University of Brighton.

Let the World Listen

by Lucie Bell

"Montpellier Crescent please," she stared blankly into the light poisoned night. The taxi driver pulled away, the sound of his spit-pumped chewing gum clacking between his teeth was louder than the engine.

"Can we put the heating on please?" She looked across at the driver with a forced smile of politeness, just another momentary lie: all part of this stained glass masquerade. How many smiles had she forged in the past eight hours? How many men had she pretended to have the hots for? How many men had she fooled into believing they had a chance at knowing her outside of that hedonistic playground?

He blasted the heat to full, stuffing the cab with artificial thick air. She'd left her makeup on and her corset on. Her red silk one, the one that made her look like some statuesque mannequin from a period drama, her malignant beauty captivated them all. She should take all this tack off really, he hates it. He hates those shitty false nails that protrude from her elegant fingers like absurd growths of a galaxy compressed into a claw of plastic. He hates those dark false eyelashes that shade her vermillion eyes like a duchess playing coquettishly with her mask at a masquerade. It felt more real despite the artificiality. If she stripped her uniform off before she greeted him, it would be like erasing the night she'd just worked.

"Eight pound forty please," his Indian voice rose out of the darkness like a hermit emerging from its shell. She left him a tenner and jumped out. There he was, she knew he'd be standing in the cold waiting for her. That pensive stare and relaxed stance sent a shiver through her body. Her James Dean, her Rossetti, her David Gandy, her Von Tripps, her Mahatma Ghandi. He didn't belong to her at all. But if he did, he was all of these people, and more. Tonight, whilst she slept, he would paint her. First he would immortalise that shoulder, that elegant and disturbingly beautiful collarbone and neck. He was a man with graphite fingers. To him, she was his muse; he wanted her to be more than that. But how could he possibly ever hope to retrieve such a *perdido Angele*? That was her appeal anyway wasn't it? Her depth, her heady mixture of sexual allure and malignant beauty, with that ever present innocent calm that hung around her form permanently. There was no way he could capture all of this on a canvas.

He put down the graphite and traced his grey stained fingers gently across her collarbone, leaving a smooth smudge of dark against her light, thin skin.

Hi, I'm Lucie Belle and I study English literature at Sussex University. I'm 20 years old and have never had any fictional writing published before. When I have more free time I'd like to write more.

Raindrop

by Michael Jones

I watch as the first raindrop collides with the window,
my eyes are compelled to meet it···*"Hello"*, I say, and I
smile.
I wonder how far you have travelled
just to greet me this morning, I wonder, how many times
you have been.

Maybe you were once an icicle, or a glacier, longing for
the cauldron of man's industrial age,
when smog and cities will release you from crystalline
bondage.
I remember you from a tatty old picture of a negro slave
ship,
sanguine and trickling from the bite of the whip.

Perhaps you were the first tear of a child,
perhaps you were the spit on the tongue of a long dead
dictator.
Now, in this tiny version of reality, you are candescent, a
droplet of liquid life.
But just as you, I have never been here in this form,
I have never known this time.

And still I wonder where your journey began.

The baying mob outside, and the raindrop have never met,
the voices now too many to count, one hundred, maybe
more?
But a miniaturised version of their image, is now held
captive in the spherical microcosm,
viewed through this tiny bubble, my bubble, and so they
fade.
And I could live inside of you, a sort of symbiotic refugee.

In warm, salty soothing currents we have touched before,
but I now await you in another guise, carrying your lethal
chemical passengers,
that plot the mapping of my veins.

I chose this though, when I married her to the water.
Mental cellulose imagery pours forth again at a mechanical
pace,
triggers my endocrine response, and I sag.
I'm playing solitaire with the only movie in the picture-
house, and she is my infinite loop.

Tendrils creep out of her scalp as she studies the riverbed,
I hold my breath and pinch my nose hard, then submerge.
So as we share our final ebbing rhythm, and climax in cold
tranquillity,
I ask her, did you love him, as you once loved me?

Then she was gone.
And now the raindrop is gone too.

While I'm led away, a spectrum of light solarises the
skyline,
as I witness Richard Of York Giving Battle In Vain for the
last time.
And as I behold my own illumination, I ask,
will I become a raindrop too?

*I am a Paramedic, currently undertaking the Mentorship
Preparation Module at Falmer. Writing is my passion, and
use it to channel my creative energies into something
tangible. I have had a few articles published, some
poetry, but haven't entered many competitions. This is
my first one for ages! I am about 55K words into my first
novel, which is a crime thriller based around the Bolivian
drug cartels.*

97

Lucky

by Mickey Cuddihy

Anna says she always has good luck followed by bad (or vice-versa, if you want to see it that way).

"Always", she says, in her slightly halting Swedish accent, "good things are happening to my work when my boyfriend breaks up with me".

This has happened several times, so her work – she is a photographic and video artist – has been going leaps and bounds, with occasional blips when she and Christian get back together again.

"You know", she says, "I managed to get a flat, in Stockholm, and this is very difficult – it is not easy to find a flat in Stockholm. I managed to get a flat, very nice, and then it got; how do you say when water comes in?"

"Flooded", I say.

"Yes, flooded, everywhere, water coming from people's flats upstairs, the plumbing. There was shit pouring down the walls; everything was ruined; the floor had to be replaced. The walls had to be re-painted".

Anna had to move out for weeks, she said. She stayed with Christian, and of course that didn't go very well, but her work was going leaps and bounds. She was nominated for a prestigious fellowship, but just as she was finishing her application – she'd gone across the road to get a cup of coffee – she was knocked down by a bus. It was February.

"Was there snow"? I ask, (wanting a picture).

"No, there was not snow, but it was cold, so (luckily) I was wearing my fur hat, and that saved my head" (Her hat sits unworn on top of the wardrobe in the room she rents from me in London – even now, in the middle of January, it hasn't been cold enough for her to wear it).

Anna was knocked unconscious, and woke later, people crowded round her. She felt great, she said, "like when you smoke marijuana, how do you say?" (Turning her finger round and round her head).
"Concussion", I say (realising later that she meant "dizzy").

"Exactly", she says. "Anyway, I went home in a taxi, and finished my application and handed it in; then I went afterwards to the hospital to have my head x-rayed"

(She was fine).

"I won the scholarship, and here I am" (studying for an MA in London).

"Once", she said, "I bought my boyfriend, Christian a beautiful bike for his birthday. I had to travel out of town to buy it, and I had to – how do you say to drive a bicycle?"

"Cycle", I say.

"Yes, I had to cycle it into Stockholm in the rain; it was raining cats and dogs, and it took me 3 hours practically; it was a beautiful bike, but then, just as I got to Christian's flat, I crashed the bike and ruined it".

Anna went back to Stockholm recently for her award ceremony, and Christian broke up with her again, but when she came back to London she received a letter inviting her to take part in an important exhibition at the Kunsthalle.

Mikey Cuddihy was born in New York. After the death of both her parents (in separate car accidents), she and four of her siblings were sent to England where she attended Summerhill, a small progressive school in Suffolk. Her memoir A Conversation About Happiness is published by Atlantic Books in April 2014. Mikey is a senior lecturer in Fine Art, Painting at University of Brighton.

Lashan Hara

by Mickey Grant

My corrupted Yiddish tongue
littered with your hard fricatives
the alveolars stick in my lungs
the word taste like swine
an oral circumcision
every no sounds like a nien!

Spitting in my Gethsemane
you call me Müller
Issac of Germany
eins zwei drei...Kike
I'm feeling more Arian today
the eyes bluer the hair almost white

When the cock shrieks
I will deny I know myself
Torah torn Boychik baptised
pissing in my Gethsemane
you call me Müller
Judas of Protestant Germany

Downsizing Radial City

by Paul Green

January 27

I have lived all my life in Radial City. So its intricate topography is etched into my memory. Every day since my retirement I leave my modest dwelling in the Bungalow District, near Monastery Gardens tram depot, and saunter through the labyrinth of lanes around Tompion Mansions, until I find myself on Progression Avenue. From here I stroll towards the City centre via Old Beaverdale Road, resisting the temptation to visit the Hospitality District and the dubious delights of Baphomet Street. I then cut across The Mire, ignoring the ribald shouts of the Rurals slaughtering their hogs, and eventually arrive at the colonnades of Snelgrove Parade, encircling the cultural hub of the City – the golden dome of the Basilica, the Polyphonic Hall, the Medusa Gallery.

Here I can sup spiced chocolate at the Café Irreal or peruse the Daily Telegram at the Café Bourgeois. The walk takes about half an hour, although today I was pleased to find that I'd done it in twenty-three minutes, despite shortness of breath and the damned walking-stick. Memo: must buy new great-coat. These armpits are too tight.

February 3

A rather uneasy evening at Edgar's. He is my only surviving friend so I do make an effort to keep in touch, even if it does involve navigating the precipitous steps down to his small tower-house behind Haddock Street. We used to reminisce about wines and women but in recent months he has become obsessed with the model tramway layout that fills his cramped attic. I have to admit I was impressed. In addition to modelling our trams, in the exact shade of ultramarine blue, with working trolley poles that sparkle along a web of overhead wires, he has created a panorama of the whole City.

'It's extraordinary!' I exclaimed. 'You've included the trading pyramids of the Fatlands, you've even re-created the Bureau, with all its turrets. Very brave...'

'I was worried about the Bureau,' he admitted. 'I know one's not supposed to take photos of it, but I thought a model in the privacy of one's home might pass un-noticed. Anyway, look what I've done with the Hospitality District.'

He handed me a magnifying glass. I peered over his miniaturisation of Baphomet Street, admiring the flickering blue neon of Uncle Bonnie's Nuderama, the cracked portico of the Tiberius Hotel, all reproduced with meticulous fidelity. Then, adjusting the lens, I studied the tiny figures – one especially, under the hotel awning.

She was recreated in exquisite detail, in her prime – the wide eyes, delicate lips, her favourite white leather coat. 'Claudia – Claudia Netherwood... How on earth did you..?'

'You rhapsodised enough about her at the funeral. Just a tiny memento for us, old friend...' He poured another thimbleful of liqueur. 'To Claudia, who expanded our youthful horizons...'

I needed to change the subject quickly; and pointed to a tram rounding the corner of Mobius

Street into Atlantis Terrace. 'The radius of that curve is rather tight, isn't it?'

He tugged his beard, obviously irritated. 'I assure you, Cedric, I have built everything to exact scale. When the Bureau downsized me last year, I ah "borrowed" some official City plans.'

I tried to disguise my alarm at his recklessness and focused on his representation of the Bungalow District, where I discovered my bijou domicile, every broken tile rendered with exactitude. However I didn't want to further antagonise him by commenting on how the bungalows seemed compressed, even slightly skewed – or how he'd omitted a model of myself.

With forced bonhomie we drank another toast to Claudia and made awkward farewells. I nearly got lost on the way home. The high walls around Tompion Mansions seemed to curve more sharply, misleading me via Trumpet Alley. Most confusing. And I must change these bloody boots.

February 10

This last week has been exhausting. I have never suffered from claustrophobia before, but now the confines of my study have become oppressive. I strain my eyes scanning the small print of my Radial City Historical Society Journals, but the shelved tomes are virtually walling me in, as if I was imprisoned in my own past.

Yesterday I tried to distract myself by opening my secret drawer of Claudia's old letters, but her minute adorable calligraphy only exacerbated my sense of entrapment. Was there room for passion, Cedric, in your microcosm of scholarship and daily routine? Now I am with Edgar – After decades, I could still feel that steely claw squeezing my heart. I must get out of the house.

February 13

I know now I should never have gone. He was drunk, in his pajamas at noon, bewildered by my surprise appearance. 'You're shrinking the City,' I shouted. 'I can feel it. You've turned everything into a toyshop, you toyed with the woman I loved!.'

'She liked toys,' he said, leering. 'Big boy's toys...' Picking up the tiny icon of Claudia between his cracked fingernails, he pressed it to his lips. 'I can still savour her taste, you know...'

The taunt was too much. I tried to snatch the precious object from him, to protect her from his foul saliva, but he twisted my arm, kicked my gammy leg... For a second we teetered, two old man wrestling with our rival memories, and then I crashed down into Radial City, cracking the fragile plastic dome of the Basilica and shattering the balsa wood façade of the Tiberius Hotel.

He screamed at the destruction, swinging a punch at me as I rose, only to throw me off-balance again, so that I crushed the roof of the Café Bourgeois and demolished all the tram wiring along Snelgrove Parade. When he bit me in the thigh, tears trickling down his cheeks, I had no option but to grab the central surveillance tower of the Bureau and bring it down on his skull.

Shortly afterwards neighbours called the security forces.

The Bureau operative dealing with my case has been polite but cold. He seems almost indifferent to Edgar's death but very concerned that an ex-employee had constructed a replica of the building from purloined plans and I had sacrilegiously destroyed it. 'That's causing serious offence,' he warned me, issuing my bail papers.

So now I huddle under a blanket on my study sofa, waiting for the Bureau agent to deliver my final summons. Wherever I'm going, keeping a journal will not be feasible. But I will clutch Claudia tightly in my pocket, even as space and time contract around me...

Paul Green is an Academic Support Worker at UoB Hastings. Work published or broadcast includes poetry, radio drama and novels, most recently Beneath The Pleasure Zones (Mandrake of Oxford). Other Radial City stories have appeared in magazines and in Unthology 2 (Unthank Books)

Love
by Phoebe Cooper

Your skin is a gift

Like many things

Except it's

What you live in

*I am a 24-year-old Cultures, Histories, Literatures
student living in London.*

Melancholy
by Claire Huber

Come to me, oh gallant angel,
Where I lay and yearn for you,
Steady my heart with your tender touch,
Ease my torment with our love so true.
Overjoyed, while feeling despair,
These emotions to me, all new,
Pleasure merged with pain, nothing forsaken,
All sweetest reminders, of you.
Oh to touch your face,
To whisper words so true,
Constantly feeling tearful,
All of my love for you.

The Lovers in the Dark

by Rachel Smith

She didn't like Helen. She didn't like her cheerful voice or the way she smelled, as if she had spent the journey smoking and then tried to cover it up with Chanel No. 5. She disliked her condescending tone and she could tell by the distraction in her voice that she wasn't paying full attention.

"Helen," she'd say, "Why did you decide to work for me?" The answer was of the usual sort, the sort that she had heard on so many occasions that it would be almost possible to recite the answer along with the speaker.

"I enjoy working with people and helping them achieve their personal goals. I enjoy watching progress." *Progress.* That's what she'd said. Well, she certainly wouldn't be seeing a lot of that here.

The room fell silent. They sat like that for a long while, Helen fiddling with the hem of her dress, rubbing it between her fingers to give them something to do. She heard the clink of the tea cup as Helen shuffled in her chair, evidently trying hard to make as little noise as possible and probably looking everywhere but at the old woman sat in front of her. She always found it drily amusing how, even around the blind, people are still afraid to stare.

***

Ezra Thompson rang on Tuesday morning. She could still hear the dance in his voice.

"It's been a while," he said. She could hear his smile before he let out a small chuckle of nervous laughter. "I'm probably the last person you thought would call," he began.

"Yes," she answered. She didn't know what else to say.

"It's just I was passing by the old hall down by the pond and I thought of you."

She felt warmth spread through her chest for a moment and heat rise in her cheeks. Unconsciously she covered her face with her hands before realising he couldn't see her.

"I wondered," he continued, "if it would be alright for me to pop in?" He began trailing off nervously, explaining how it had been so long since they had seen each other and how they both had so much to catch up on. As he talked she found herself wondering where he was calling from, she could hear the slight crackle in the line and imagined him on the other end, the chord wound around his arm, or one of his hands. She wondered if perhaps he was calling from his own phone and, like her, was sitting alone in his lounge. Or perhaps he wasn't alone. She gripped the handset tightly, wondering if the silence behind his voice was the presence of another. Did he ever marry? She didn't know. Had he had children? She didn't know that either.

"Anyway, I just thought it would be nice to see you"
he finished breaking her from her thoughts.

"Yes," she replied. That seemed to be all she could
say.

"So it's alright if I come to visit?" he asked.
"Yes," she replied, "yes."

He hung up then and she felt a sudden fear that he
would appear in front of her that very instant. It was
a juvenile fear but she felt it all the same. Placing the
phone back down she let her hand rest lightly on top
of it, as if she were holding the last remnants of him.
He had thought of her was all she could think. After
all of this time, he had thought of her.

***

She remembered it had been a cold night, she could
see her breath curling up into the blackness.
Following him outside she had felt a strange relief
leaving the noise of the hall behind her. He had
moved faster than she anticipated and as he
disappeared around the side of the building she had
whispered his name into the darkness. He replied
with a cough and, trailing her fingers over the
uneven stone surface of the wall, she made her way
towards him. The ground was wet beneath her feet,
sucking at her shoes with every step. She moved
slowly,

"Don't worry" he said, his voice travelling towards

her, "it only takes a moment for your eyes to adjust." She paused, allowing the sound of his footsteps to stop in front of her. "I can't see you" she said, squinting her eyes as if it might help. She could just make out his silhouette, his tall frame set against the wideness of his shoulders, the size of his hands as he lifted them towards her face.

"Can you see me now?" he asked, clasping her face in his hands, blocking all sound coming from the dance hall. It seemed to her as if the world had stopped. It was quiet, safe. He leaned into her, the weight of his body naturally moving her to fall back against the wall that only moments before, had guided her to him. His body was heavy against hers, his heat seeping through the thin material of her dress, spreading over her skin. She was shaking with expectancy, her eyes on his lips, anticipating them to crash onto hers at any moment. She heard the music inside start up again, another dance beginning. She imagined her mother inside, stopping to look around the room, interrupting her friends and asking if they had seen her daughter, moving over to her father and questioning him. A smile played on Ezra's lips.

She couldn't help feeling a delighted sense of abandon as she leant forward to kiss him, aware that any moment Prissy could round the corner, or her father, or even her mother. He kissed her back, his hungry mouth wet against hers and tangy with alcohol. He tugged roughly at the dress her mother had sewn for her, almost as anxious to remove it as she had been this morning when she had been forced to try it on. He felt hot between her legs and, in a

111

move of sudden desperation she tugged her dress up to her waist as he closed the space between them. Against that wall in the darkness, with a man she only knew the name of she couldn't help but laugh. If only her mother could see her now.

Rachel Smith is a third year English Literature student, studying at the University of Brighton. Throughout her degree she has focused on developing her creative writing and constantly pushing her narrative boundaries. She is currently pursuing applications for a Masters Degree where she hopes to further explore the reading, writing, and publication process.

Weather

by Robyn Nightingale

You are 17 when you meet the love of your life.
She is warm waves lapping at your ankles,
soft fingers threading through your hair,
a voice like autumn leaves lulling you to sleep.

When you are 19 you have a bitter wind inside you.
You become a marine in hopes that it will warm your numb
fingers
but can never find it in yourself to regret it–
even when you leave and your fingers are black with frost
bite,
phantom pains where your left leg used to be.

When you are 20, everything is okay.
You return home with a brand-new prosthetic and not
much else.
The house is empty,
the fridge is off, dust has gathered on the coffee table and
the house is empty.
Dead branches rake at your insides, catch in your skin.
You try to believe it when you whisper
everything is okay.

She finds you in the shower.
You'd slipped –prosthetics don't grip well in water–
and hadn't gotten up since.

She brushes your hair from your forehead,
touches fingertips against your temples and says,
voice cracking like autumn leaves,
everything is okay
and you think you might believe her.

I have in no way experienced a real war. I do however
know what it's like to have a bitter wind that festers
inside you.

Denise's World

by Sarah George

At first glance she was the earth-shatteringly average type
of woman
The vicar reeled off mundane job after mundane job
Assistant Marketer
Customer Assistant
Clerk
Sales Temp
Personal Assistant
Like this was all that she consisted of
As if her world were just as tiny and humdrum as her job
titles

I seethe and protest
This is not, cannot be, all that she really is
Because I really knew her, and she stretched out as if
infinite, boundless

She is every smile that she planted on the face of another
Innumerable stretches and twirls carved out at fitness
classes
A deluge of hair-salon receipts for root retouching
Skilfully crafted cups of coffee, one for every day of her
working life
Millions of scrawls left by trademark sparkly pens in
greetings cards
Endless hugs and kisses which she blessed her loved ones
with
Box upon box of beautiful decorations selected for her
Christmas-tree masterpieces
Countless smiles forced as the cancer fought violently
within her
Each lily-bloom that sat prettily upon her little home for
the rest of eternity

Everything she had touched still glows with the essence of
her
And since she passed I see her in seemingly everything I
lay eyes upon
I hear her in the melody of every song she used to sing
with my mother
I feel her in the comfort of a warm blanket's hug
I smell her in the aroma of freshly- brewed coffee

I realise that her scope is not small in the slightest
That her world continues infinitely
That it keeps on turning and orbiting
Even when the rest of us can't see her within it anymore.

*My name is Sarah George and I am a current first year
undergraduate studying a joint honours BA in English
Language and English Literature at Sussex University. I
love creative writing in my free time, as well as working
to create journalistic pieces for the Sussex Tab and the
Badger.*

He Who Always Treads in Sandals

by Sean Fitzsimons

Hasn't seen his bearded friend,
since 79 in a two-man tent,
they exchange words,
a flask of coffee,
nostalgia? No,
not these old bodies
He who always treads in sandals

Just one return
to the outback shed,
no family to greet,
a pension to collect
sinks a schooner extra dry,
takes up the sack
looks to the sky
He who always treads in sandals

Witnessed the notes,
first played on the beach,
with some Germans on boats,
but he'll never return,
the bohemian toasts
"to good fucking times"
He who always treads in sandals

More clinking of bottles,
drinking of sorrows,
than the average drunk,
his stories they borrow,
from one to another,
a waterless pirate
He who always treads in sandals

Hammock rocks gently,
cradled by wind,
the ceiling hook earth,
spins and sings,
not a new day,
but a final destination
He who always treads in sandals

Sean Fitzsimons, 21, Studying English Language &
Linguistics
Writes about music, people and places. Written for The
Source Brighton, The Tab Sussex,
ThisIsOurTownKingston and Lindfield Arts Festival.

Sigourney Weaver

by Sean Flemming

It's times like these You can feel the hearts in
everyone's chest
   beating with choral vigour and the
      Blood coursing through their veins.

I look around and Everyone in Victoria Park is eating
their ice cream

   just for me.

Trees shimmer and pulse with life,

   and ripple within their skin whilst

The poolwater scintillates, twinkles like an ocean of
conflict diamonds
   As children splash their parents for attention.

Old men contemplate their sundown years in
sunbaked hats
     and
   Single mothers forget their troubles for the
moment.

Dogs bark pleasantries, but we can't hear,
   I see smiles passed on like a relay baton, around
and around the Olympic track of

   Right now.

Young women float on by like clouds wearing
summer dresses and with a little help from the sun
        I can make out the outlines of their thighs.

This must be what it's like to make love to the
universe,
I think –

Just as the scenery falls away and I find myself
        on stage with roses at my feet and a smiling
crowd and
Sigourney Weaver handing me an award for

        "MOST PASSIVE OBSERVER"

There is so much applause that I barely notice

        the squirrel darting up my shoulder

and telling me next week's lottery numbers.

Half Past Eight

by Sina Krause

I have never talked to him until that morning. He is
my half past eight. That is what I call him in my head.
Sometimes I add a mister. Ah, Mister Half Past Eight
is here. If he could hear my thoughts, he would think
I am mad. When he enters, I know I have twenty
minutes before I have to leave. He comes in ten
minutes after me, orders his coffee and sits at one of
the tables in the corner. But the café was packed that
day. He looked around wondering who to approach
and share a table with. He chose me. Given that I am
aware of his existence, he most likely was aware of
mine. To him I might be the woman in the work
uniform clutching her cup of coffee and book. "May
I?" he asked. "Sure" I said. He sat down, briefly
smiled at me and opened his paper. We read silently,
until it was time for me to go. He looked up. "This
may sound weird, but you are my ten to nine" he said.
"I'm what?" I asked, yet I knew exactly what he
meant.

*Sina has dedicated her writing to stories where nothing
happens. She will stay stuck in this ponderous
existentialism, until the first comedy forces itself through
all the doom and gloom. She joined forces with The-Ed-
W-Approach, where the practice of writing merges with
video, performance and critical practice: The-Ed-W-
Approach.co.uk*

Perception Deception
by Steven Dumaresq

Trapped inside the illusion of reality
Conditioned by the perception of insanity,
Consumerist ideals, obedience and vanity
And perpetrated agendas of profanity

Emancipate yourself within the divinity
Liberate your soul through the holy trinity,
Altruistic values and acts of affinity
Through the universe into infinity

Mankind bound by the theory of gravity,
Pre-conceived notions of morality disparity
Believe in the liberation of humanity
Free your mind and fly through the galaxy.

BANG

by Sue Rumens

BANG!

Like a pistol.

So close to the little boy's face, she was sure he would be traumatized.

The look on the man's face was determined, deliberate – almost demonic.

She heard herself cry out: 'Please – don't burst them all.'

He didn't acknowledge her, but his hands loosened their grip. The remaining balloons were pushed high onto the draining board, out of the child's reach.

Silence.

No-one moved. The other adults didn't intervene – the children were stunned.

Then the child burst into tears.

She wanted to go and console him but she was taut – stretched in all directions.

Guilt, for allowing it to happen, competed with some misguided attempt to justify it.

Her overwhelming and unconditional love for the child made his suffering so hard to bear.

She looked at the wrinkled orange remnant that was the balloon. Then she moved away from the sink and began to pick up some of the other toys strewn around the floor.

They had been having such a jolly time.

Yes, the children had been getting a little excited, running around and screeching. But it was Halloween – the house decorated with spiders, pumpkins and ghostly ghouls.

Her grandson could be a handful, but she knew his parents were taking a 'three strikes and you're out' approach. If he didn't respond, he would be removed from whatever he was doing to spend five minutes on the 'naughty step'.

But to deliberately burst his balloon – right in his face like that?

It was akin to something a mean older brother might do to his younger sibling – like pulling the wheels from a favourite toy train.

What level of jealousy had turned the man into a vindictive monster?

Who was this person she had shared her life with for the past ten years?

She always tried to make things right. It's what she did – what she was good at.

At work, she was the one people came to when they were in despair. After a chat, with a cup of tea and a box of tissues, she sent them away happier than when they arrived. Problem not necessarily solved, but the mood lightened – and the reassurance of knowing where she was next time.

So, for the sake of harmony, she tried to act as if nothing had happened.

She painted on a tight smile, grateful for her glasses which were going someway to conceal her tear filled eyes.

She became conscious that, all around her, conversation was cautiously resuming.

After a little while the child's sobbing eased, and he found his way on to her lap.

'Granddad burst my balloon,' he wailed.

'I know,' she whispered in his ear. 'But you weren't listening to him.'

'It went BANG, like shouting.

'Yes,' she said. 'Granddad was cross because you were being naughty. Never mind. Perhaps we can find you another balloon now you're a good boy.'

He shook his head.

'No,' he said. 'My balloon is gone.'

She noticed the other children chose their own secret moment to reassure the little boy. They smiled kindly, putting an arm around him – but they kept their own balloons out of the way. Even at their tender age, they seemed to understand a line had been crossed.

She knew things were coming to a head.

They had been here before of course – the same conversation over and over. He would accuse her of putting her family first. Not denying it, she would try to reassure him that she had room in her heart for both.

But he knew – in fact she had warned him:

'Never make me choose'.

He was hardly there anyway – the cravings of a workaholic as strong as those of any other addiction. They struggled to find time to do things together. She wasn't even sure they enjoyed the same things.

And yet, things had been better for a while. He tried to participate when the grandchildren visited. Appearing to accept that this stage of her life wouldn't last forever – that there would be time for them as a couple again once the grandchildren started school.

Who could she talk to?

She couldn't speak to her children – too terrified they would stop her grandchildren from coming to her house.

A few weeks before there had been another incident. Minutes after the child had arrived, he had started to misbehave, throwing a toy across the room and so granddad had intervened. The smack on the hand sounded harder than she felt appropriate – but then was a smack ever justified?

She knew she had to deal with it – but what to say?

'Your behaviour is unacceptable – never touch my grandchild again.'

Too dramatic?

Many years before, a friend had given her advice concerning her ex-husband:

'What matters is whether you believe his actions are right or wrong. If he is crossing the parameters of what you find acceptable, then it's wrong.'

Sound advice. So why hadn't she learnt from this? Was she one of these helpless women, doomed to be a victim of some controlling man?

Suppose she did nothing and one day he gave the child a real whack?

A teacher would be cautioned for such abuse – perhaps even lose their job. Why should a step grandparent believe themselves to be above the law? For it was abuse – physical and emotional.

She must deal with it – but what to do?

Tonight the child would share his woeful tale with his parents. She would be on tender hooks waiting for their call. Why had she not intervened? They might turn up at the door, pointing an accusing finger...

Perhaps it would help to have her son there when she tackled him?

No. That was the coward's way – looking for someone else to deal with it or ignoring it and hoping it goes away.

She must have it out with him – there was no choice.

Soda Cracker

by Tabby Detroit

Mary didn't go down to the river very often these days, the older she grew the less she liked looking at her reflection in the water and although you can never step in the same river twice it was becoming more and more apparent that the only thing changing was the skin on her face. She began to wonder if her bones had aged, she considered what aging bones might look like; perhaps they became mottled and grey and brittle or perhaps they became soft, caving in on themselves like the empty husks of her idle daydreams. She wasn't quite sure when her long life had become so short. Looking back on her 80 years she could only remember fragments, it was as though everyday a cloth was thrown over her memories and every morning she must wake up and think– what's gone or rather what's left? She could remember the crisp smell of starched linen when her father hugged her as a girl. She remembered her stepmother pulling her hair into tight curls. She remembered her husband slamming his fist into the wall. Her daughters first birthday. She remembered her grandsons christening and the way the priest had shook her hand so warmly as she entered the church. She remembered bathing her baby granddaughter in the sink and she wondered when she had grown so big and if she could possibly be the same girl. But mainly she had forgotten, until her life just became a series of imprints, a Monet painting that would remain a blur until she saw it from far, far away; an aerial view.

She thought about friendship, and how far away her friends were now and if she'd get to join them soon. She asked herself what a friend was and the difference between death and loss. She concluded that both were grievous but one was irrevocable and the other was merely a choice. She thought of her choices, her shortcomings and mistakes. The moon was bright, but it had been brighter last year, the river was clear, but it had been clearer the year before, the air was fresh, no, it was stale. And she began to think of life as a little bit of stale, as a little bit of stale bread they give you at the altar when you go to church, yes, she began to think of life as a little bit of soda cracker that she was going to use up fairly quickly and not particularly enjoy. But that at least her stale little bit of life would represent the whole stinking body of humanity that will also live and be good for goods sake only to waste away and be forgotten and rebuked by the generations to follow.

This is not to say she was a martyr, just a little bit of bread, simple and unimposing.

Tabby is a young writer from London living in Brighton, her honest and grating poetry is often performed at spoken word nights in Brighton. She has been described as a writer that contrasts the ebb and flow of the urban with the impulse of the natural and instinctive.

Things I am Sorry For

by Tanaka Mhishi

The lies. All of them.
(Sometimes stories happen to me like violence.
Sometimes I say truths instead of facts.
Sometimes I want life to be easy.
It's no excuse, it's just the only explanation I
can give you.)

The wine.
(Not the first glass but the second. Third.
Fourth.)
The stain.
The bald patch on the lawn.
The broken plate.
The empty drawers.

What happened to your mother.
What happened to mine.
The day the sunshine didn't last,
when you forgot your keys
and it started to rain.

The codeine and the razor blades.
The time I stole your pain medication to get high.
The afternoon a bird kamikazeed into your
window frame
(Its kidneys blasting their sour milk over the
new paint)

The days I've inflicted my body on you.
Each time you heard me laugh.
Bringing my underdeveloped calf muscles onto
your football team.

That I turned out this way.
(Storyteller, butcher, thief,
catamite, shame spiller,
26 inch waist
smear of ego)

That I said you could fly.
That you believed me.

The mould. The odd socks. The chicken pox,
the spilled ink. The danger, the bloody asphalt,
trip to A&E. The sleepless nights. The letters
home. The unmade bed.

The lies.
I am sorry for the lies. Each one.
Even this.

*Tanaka Mhishi studies English Literature at the
University of Brighton. His first play was staged as part
of a promenade performance at the Vault festival in
March 2014. More of his work can be found at
www.tmhishi.tumblr.com*

Drowning

by Tania Turner

George sat entranced as he watched the fish gently swim about the tank through the waving plants with their delicate fronds, sometimes hiding in the carefully built caves. The hum of the pump was the only sound in the room apart from the distant roar of the traffic outside. With the lights off and the curtains drawn, it was a haven; here nothing could go wrong.

He got up and sprinkled just the right amount of fish food onto the surface. George did this at the same time each day. The fish rose to the surface pushing and shoving, trying to get the most. The water started to boil and he saw their fins and tails strangely out of place in the air, somehow not as beautiful. Sometimes he let his fingers slide down into the silky water and they came and nibbled at his flesh, soft sucking motions at his large, scarred workhands, it was almost sensuous, hurriedly he pulled out his hand wiping it dry on his old trousers.

After the phone call telling him that Gilly, his daughter had been killed in a car crash he had been numb, it was as though something had shifted inside. It felt like a hole right in the middle of his body that dragged at him as he went around the house, he was frightened that he might fall right inside and be lost.

You expected to die before your children, not the other way round, it put into doubt everything he had thought about the future, his plans. Before this had happened, he had imagined his grandchildren staying and him teaching them all the things that his father had taught him, how to saw a piece of wood, then the plane gliding with the grain and the soft crunch of shavings underfoot, the room filling with the sweet scent of pine.

After the first month had passed, he decided he would build a fish tank in the spare room. Gradually it started to take shape; he lovingly created a coral reef in the middle of a grey and wet town. When it was finished, it shone bright with flashes of oranges and purple, as the fish glided through the crystal water. As he sat and watched from his armchair with the curtains closed and the light off it glowed and his heart felt not exactly joy but a sort of pleased swelling that he had created something beautiful. Joan his wife said on seeing it for the first time:

'That's really beautiful, Gilly would have loved it.'

George found he was spending more and more time with the fish and he started to eat his meals in the room on his own. He found that he did not want to talk to Joan in case she mentioned their daughter; he could not bear it. Once you have experienced death you always expect it is going to happen again, the fear that nothing is permanent is always there.

George did not want anyone near him, he was fine on his own. He did not want to see Joan trying not to cry.

133

One day Joan started screaming at him, 'You're a selfish bastard.' Her eyes wide and hard, 'But do you know I don't care anymore, you can have your bloody fish because I'm going. I can't stand you not speaking or even looking at me, it is as though you can't bear the sight of me since Gilly died. Yes – I said her name, don't look so shocked, you can't hide or pretend it hasn't happened.'

George just looked at her and said nothing.
Her shoulders sagged, 'Well – that says everything, you can't even say goodbye.' And sadly she turned and walked away.

He moved the camp bed in front of the tank staring at the fish as he fell asleep to the hypnotic sound of the pump. The first thing he saw when he woke was them gliding about as if time had not passed. Life slowed down and it seemed as though there was nothing but him and the fish, nothing else seemed important. Then one day he caught sight of his reflection in the glass, a stranger looked back at him and he traced the outline with his fingers. An orange fish followed his movements and in a fit of rage, he punched the glass, a large cracked appeared. Horrified he quickly got a bucket and tried catching them, but the blood from his hand swirled in the water hiding them from him.

With a crack, the glass broke and the water gushed out over him and the room. Desperately he groped amid the wreckage for the gasping, writhing fish. Finally, he caught the last one and gently placed it in the now full bucket. He sank on to the sofa and held his head in his hands; George was unaware of the quiet click of the door behind him.

She came into the room very softly and lifted her hand as if not sure what to do with it. When she laid it lightly on his shoulder, George stiffened but did not turn around. Joan was just about to take her hand away when she felt his hand placed very carefully on top of hers, just brushing the skin. As she stared down at their hands, he suddenly gasped and gripped hers very tightly.

I am a mature student with children and teenagers, and in my third year of a joint honours English Language and Literature degree at Brighton University.

Afterword

The worlds in this anthology are small but powerful. Some are funny places, others are vibrant and intricate. Some of these stories are bitingly perceptive, others achingly sad, and we would like to thank our contributors, without whom this book would not exist, and to those who volunteered their time as proof-readers and editors.

We are also indebted to Isabel Ashdown, the University's writer in residence, to Dr Jess Moriarty and to Paddy Maguire for their support and advice in producing this collection.

The University of Brighton Literary Society
April 2014